A TEMPTING FRIENDSHIP

KYLIE GILMORE

Published by: Extra Fancy Books

ISBN-13: 978-1-942238-17-1

Sometimes friendship can be so tempting!

1

———

"Welcome, ladies, to the very first Singles Book Club! I'm your hostess, Hailey Adams, also known as Clover Park's one and only wedding planner! I hope to plan a wedding for each and every one of you! Now you might have noticed…"

What in the world am I doing here? Julia Turner fidgeted in her seat and glanced around the circle of six women (and zero men) gathered at Something's Brewing Café. All of them hanging on Hailey's every word. Julia had only called Hailey out of sheer desperation. She couldn't find a way forward with her best friend Angel Marino, not with their screwed-up history. Besides, Angel needed his freedom. He'd been looking after her ever since Brad died. Like she was his duty. She'd met him when she was only eighteen. Some part of him would always see her as that young girl. The only solution was for her to meet someone new, which would free Angel to find someone that truly deserved him.

Five years she'd been a widow. Five years Angel had been a devoted friend. Five years he'd been everything she wanted and everything she couldn't have—forbidden.

Hailey flicked her strawberry blond hair, her pale blue eyes bright. "Since it's just us ladies, I thought we'd open ourselves up to love with our first selection…" She paused and the women leaned in. "The Fierce trilogy!"

"Ooh!" the women chorused. Except for Julia, who was fighting a full-on body blush. When she'd met Hailey at cooking class earlier this month, Hailey seemed to intuitively understand Julia's predicament and handed her a business card, promising to help. The card read Hailey Adams, Love Junkie. Perhaps that should've been a red flag. The fact that Hailey was Clover Park's wedding planner and notorious matchmaker should've been a red flashing light of danger. But now she was stuck. Hailey was giving her the extra-special treatment because she was a widow, going out of her way to make sure she was comfortable. The woman had given her a big hug and the sympathy eyes when she'd first arrived and saved her a seat right next to her. There was really no polite way to leave.

"I heard the Fierce trilogy is so good!" Ally Bloom, a fellow teacher and friend, exclaimed from Julia's other side. Ally was blond, young, excitable—the near opposite of Julia's brunette, older than her twenty-eight years, weary self. Her friend was twenty-three and already open to new relationships after a recent breakup with her college boyfriend of four years. At that age, Julia had become a widow. Brad died a hero for his country during his last year of required army service. She'd married him at nineteen.

When Julia had mentioned the book club to Ally, her friend immediately decided they both *had* to go.

"*Fierce Longing, Fierce Craving,* and *Fierce Loving,*" Ally announced the titles of the trilogy, her voice rising with each book. "It sounds so passionate!"

Hailey piped up. "Now it *is* erotic romance, but there's no BDSM, so I hope that's okay with you ladies." She pointed at each of them, her perfectly manicured pink fingernail daring them to speak up or forever hold their peace.

Ally whispered something to the woman next to her, Lauren, who whispered back, and then they both nodded enthusiastically. In fact, every single one of the twentysomething women looking for love enthusiastically agreed. Except Mad, short for Madison, a woman with short fire-engine-red dyed hair and a black T-shirt that proclaimed Crazy Bitch.

Mad jerked her chin and said, "Whatever. I'm only here because I lost a bet." This, of course, they all knew because she'd announced when she arrived that her older brother had "suckered her into it," but she felt the need to remind them that she *really* didn't want to be here.

Mad's older brother, Josh, the charming bartender from Garner's Sports Bar & Grill, was supposed to be the token male at the book club and, as Hailey had informed them earlier, he'd failed to come through in her request to send any single male friends their way. It seemed that his usual interest in entertaining the ladies didn't extend to reading a book of Hailey's choosing.

The pink fingernail of doom hovered in Julia's direction, spiking her body temperature. She quickly busied herself looking for a ponytail holder in her purse. If she had her hair up, surely she'd cool off, this telltale blush would die down, and she could formulate a convincing response.

The circle of women—Ally, Lauren, Mad, Carrie, Charlotte, and Hailey—fell silent.

"Julia," Hailey prompted.

She jerked her head up, took in all the questioning faces, and felt a bead of sweat running down her spine. She yanked her hair into a high ponytail and pulled her sweater away from her overheated body. "What?"

Hailey gave her a small, patient smile. "Will my choice of book be okay with you? We'll be alternating fiction and nonfiction, so it won't always be smutty, *sinful*—" she paused to fan herself "—juicy stuff. This is just to make us more open to meeting someone. Getting us in the mo-o-od for love." She lifted a finger and addressed the room. "I *will* find some men for book club." She turned to Julia. "You are here because you're ready to meet someone, correct?"

Julia swallowed hard, opened her mouth and closed it again. *Incorrect.* She really wasn't ready to meet anyone, but she had to do something to fix the mess she'd made between her and Angel. Their screwed-up history was all on her. She'd crossed the line; she had to fix it.

Sex ruined everything.

Sleeping with Angel the night of Brad's funeral had been the worst mistake of her life. Even worse than the first time she'd slept with Angel. The guilt and shame over that, both times, had been overwhelming, but what nearly killed her was Angel bailing on her. Both times. Everyone important in her life bailed on her—her birth mom, Brad, and, worst of all, Angel.

The last time they'd screwed had nearly destroyed their friendship. Nearly destroyed her. Angel stopped visiting, only called, and when they talked, he was distant. She didn't see him for an excruciating month. Between the loss of Brad and the loss of Angel, she thought she would die. When Angel finally did stop by, he was so closed off, barely looking at her, no trace of the old teasing Angel around.

He hadn't touched her since, not even in a friendly gesture. Five long years. She knew he must've regretted it as much as she did.

They could never cross that line again. Forbidden.

She blinked as Hailey squatted in front of her in a pink cashmere sweater and pink pants, looking directly into Julia's eyes. Hailey spoke in a careful, measured tone like Julia might freak out at any minute. "How about we just read the first chapter of the first book, *Fierce Longing*, out loud to see if it works for you. Would that be okay?"

Julia's palms were sweating. She never liked to be the center of attention. She focused on Hailey's pink shoulder, unable to sustain the direct eye contact. She was no prude. She just wasn't quite prepared for…this.

"Come on, Julia," Ally called. "Don't be such a good girl."

Julia was *not* a good girl. It was a shameful, painful fact that she had to live with.

"No shaming, ladies," Hailey announced, rising to her feet and taking them all in. "We all have personal circumstances that may be, uh, personal."

"Can we just get on with this?" Mad asked, slouching further in her chair and crossing her black work boots over each other. "I'm so bored I could spit."

"There's no call for that," Hailey said primly. She took her seat and pursed her pink lips. "We would've liked to see your brother here today."

Mad rolled her eyes. "Everyone wants to see my brother." She looked around the café. "Any chance I can get a cup of joe?"

"Please do," Hailey said. "Anyone else want a drink while I chat with Julia?"

Julia stiffened. She did *not* want to have a probing heart-to-heart with Miss Perky. "I'm sure whatever book you picked will be just fine."

"Yay!" Ally did a little clap of glee.

Ten minutes later, everyone settled with their drinks. Hailey stood, holding an e-reader, behind Julia's chair. "Ready for *Fierce Longing*? If you all like it, we can get the other two books too."

"Hold up," Charlotte, a personal trainer wearing a long black tunic and black yoga pants, said. "Is this a cliffhanger?"

"I think so," Hailey said. "It's the same couple in all three."

"Now we have to read all three," Charlotte moaned.

The other ladies grumbled about not having the whole story up front. Julia shifted in her seat. Were they really going to spend three weeks of book club getting turned on...together? When she'd signed up for a singles book club, she hadn't imagined getting turned on in front of a bunch of women. She'd pictured polite conversation with single men, helped along by Hailey's cheerful prompts. This was going to be so embarrassing. But then Hailey began to read in her clear, crisp tones, and she made the story come to life.

Damon Ryder was an ordinary man with extraordinary powers of persuasion. He brokered deals that could not be brokered, negotiated the nonnegotiable, and brought his talents equally to whatever woman he wanted. And, this time, he wanted librarian Mia Lilly. He didn't care that she was his best friend's little sister, a dewy innocent twenty-two to his thirty, unused to the rougher passions. He'd wanted her before she left for college, and now that she'd returned home, he'd have her. Damon Ryder took what he wanted.

Julia crossed her legs tightly and avoided eye contact with the other women.

Hailey went on in a hushed voice. *He waited in the shadows outside of the library for Mia. She strode at a brisk pace down the sidewalk, her purse held tightly in one hand as she made her way to her car. Damon grabbed her from behind and pulled her into the shadows, quickly muffling her scream with his hand.* Hailey lowered her voice to a husky tone that approximated a man startlingly well. *"Mia, you know me. Come with me." He did not ask, he demanded, expecting full compliance.*

The throbbing between Julia's legs intensified. It had been five years since she'd been with a man.

Hailey went on. *He turned her to face him. Mia's hand flew to her throat, but he could see the hidden banks of desire in her wide brown eyes. He knew what she longed for, what she craved.*

"Damon, you scared me." Hailey's voice played a breathy feminine tone. The woman should've been an actress. *Damon wrapped her long, dark brown hair around his fist. "That was not my intent." He didn't miss the flush to her cheeks, nor her rapid breathing. He tilted her head, using his grip on her hair to expose her pale throat. Her scent, roses and intoxicating Mia, filled him with lust. He placed his lips on the rapidly beating pulse of her neck, and she let out a tiny gasp. He lifted his head, still holding her in a tight grip. "Get in the car, Mia. It's time."*

"T-time for what?"

"Time to satisfy this fierce longing," Damon growled.

"Oh," she said on a shaky breath. She licked her lips, the movement drawing his attention, quickening his pulse.

"Do you deny me?" Damon demanded.

"No."

He guided her to the car, settling her in with great care, and took off. The Ferrari, like the man, roared with barely leashed power. "Do you remember your safe word?"

"Where are we going?" Mia squeaked.

"We're going to my estate, where you will learn the depth of your passion and I will slake mine. We can only do this if I know you remember the word you chose upon your return to Longwood. Say it and everything stops."

Hailey paused.

"Keep going!" the women chorused. Except Julia, who was soaked with desire and a fierce longing just like the book's title. Having Hailey behind her made it surprisingly easy to get into the story. The voices felt so real, the tension, the attraction. She kept her gaze fixed on a small dark knot in the wood of the floor, not wanting the other women to notice how flushed she felt.

Hailey placed a hand on Julia's shoulder, making her jump. "Are you okay so far, Julia? I don't want to make anyone uncomfortable."

Julia shook her head, her cheeks burning. "I'm fine!" she squeaked. "Don't worry about me. This is fine. Great. No problem at all."

"Sure?" Hailey asked.

"Just get on with it!" Mad barked.

Hailey continued with the darkly erotic scene that took place on Damon's luxury dining room table, followed by a shared bath to soothe Mia before the ultimate seduction in his bedroom, where he'd never allowed another woman before. Mia didn't use her safe word even once. Julia wouldn't have either. Not with a man like Damon. She pushed a sweaty tendril of hair off her forehead just as Hailey announced, "And that's chapter one, ladies. Read on your own and we'll chat about it at our next meeting in two weeks."

There was no way in hell Julia was going to "chat" about something that got her off like this book did. If she'd been alone, she very well might've—

"Or we could go right to the nonfiction choice," Hailey said in a tone that said *the boring choice*. She took her seat again next to Julia. "It's called *Rejuvenate Your Life Through Decluttering*. It might be good before the New Year." New Year's Day was only two days away.

"Boo," the women chorused.

"I'd like that one, please," Julia said, earning a groan from her fellow single women looking for love.

Hailey held up a hand. "I want everyone to feel comfortable. We'll do the nonfiction choice next time as Julia requested. Please read *Fierce Longing* on your own, if you like." She flashed a quick grin. "I sure will."

The women gathered their purses and coats. Ally gave Julia a small smile. "I'll let you know how *Fierce Longing* is. Maybe you'll change your mind."

"No, that's okay," Julia said, avoiding eye contact as her cheeks and neck burned. "You just enjoy it on your own. I'm going to grab that other book. See ya." She hurried through the archway that led to the attached bookstore.

"Happy New Year!" Ally called.

"You too!" she returned with a quick glance over her shoulder. Ally waved jauntily with a big smile and headed out the door with the other women. Julia tried to think cooling thoughts as she went to the nonfiction section.

Hailey appeared at her side. "I hope I haven't offended you."

Far from it. "Not at all," Julia replied sincerely. "I'm just much more interested in nonfiction." *Not really.* She grabbed the book that was face-out, *Rejuvenate Your Life Through Decluttering*, and under that title was a bold promise in big letters, "Add joy to your life!" Julia stared at it for a moment, hoping it was true. She could really use some joy in her life. A part of her died with her husband, Brad. Even his name, Turner, stuck with her, a constant reminder. Even though it would be easier to go back to her maiden name, MacKendrick, some part of her couldn't sully his memory by slashing away his name. She wouldn't be the person she was today without him. His extroverted, energetic personality had brought her out of her shell, introducing her to a party lifestyle, a social life she'd never had before. She'd spent most of high school at home reading; sometimes she read side-by-side with her equally introverted best friend. She rarely went out, never had a boyfriend. In college, with Brad at her side, she'd connected with people for the first time. Her throat got tight. Dammit. She definitely needed rejuvenation.

She glanced at Hailey, who smiled. The woman reminded Julia of a beautiful princess from a fairy tale. The kind that would sing to the forest animals. "I'll go pay for this."

She took the book to the register, and Hailey followed. It seemed Hailey wasn't done with her yet.

"Find everything you need today?" the woman behind the register asked. She had dark brown hair in a braid and black-rimmed glasses. She looked a little like Julia imagined the bookish Mia, minus the glasses.

"Yes, thank you," Julia said.

"Anything else?" the woman prompted. "We have the Fierce trilogy in paperback."

Julia flushed and shook her head.

Hailey piped up. "If you change your mind, you can buy the e-book."

"I'm fine," Julia said, forcing a smile for Hailey and the other woman's benefit. She handed over her credit card. A few minutes later, book in hand, she headed out, Hailey hot on her heels.

"All sexy books aside," Hailey said in a low tone, "you do want help changing your single status, don't you? I mean, that's why you called me. Everyone else showed up here today because of a flyer I posted in the bookstore, except Mad and your friend. Anyway, I got the feeling you really needed my help."

Julia stopped and took a deep breath, her stomach already tightening with anxiety. "Yes, I guess so."

"It won't be hard to find someone who wants to take you out. I mean, look at you!" Hailey lifted a lock of Julia's hair. "Gorgeous long chestnut brown hair—"

"It's just dark brown and shoulder length."

Hailey went on as if Julia hadn't spoken. "With blue eyes and flawless skin, a captivating combination!" Julia flushed as Hailey continued to wax poetic, waving her hands all around Julia like she was showing off the features of the newest sports car. "High cheekbones, adorable little pointed chin, and I know you've got curves hiding—"

"Hailey, I'm begging you, lower your voice. And your hands."

Hailey dropped her hands and asked in a fervent whisper that surely carried throughout the store, "You remember Josh from cooking class? Mad's older brother the bartender?"

Julia nodded. Josh was handsome, but extremely flirty with all women. Clearly experienced and used to playing the field. She wasn't ready for the likes of Josh. "I don't think Josh is a good choice for me."

Hailey leaned in conspiratorially. "You can practice on him. He thought you were pretty, and he's not looking for serious. Could be fun, right? A good icebreaker to step back into the dating pool?"

And, though Julia could surely use the practice (she'd only ever dated her husband), she feared Josh was just too big of a first step. "I don't think so."

Hailey put a polished pink finger to her pink lips and studied Julia.

"Thanks anyway," Julia said in what she hoped was a breezy but firm tone. "I should be going." It was difficult enough to get up the nerve to go to Singles Book Club without Hailey insisting on a setup with Josh. Besides, Julia was still revved up from that sexy first chapter. She needed to take the edge off with her trusty vibrator, Bob the III, far away from other women.

She took a step toward the door when Hailey stopped her with a hand on her arm. "Clover Park doesn't have a lot of single men. At least, none that I'm acquainted with. Why don't you cast a wider net?" Hailey pressed a small folded piece of paper into Julia's hand. "It's an online dating site that comes highly recommended."

Julia held the paper with the tips of her fingers like it was on fire. "Oh, I don't know…online dating doesn't seem all that safe." And the thought of meeting up with a stranger made her nauseous.

Hailey snagged the paper and shoved it into the gap at the top of Julia's purse. "You meet them in a public place and let a friend know where and when you'll be meeting them. It's just as safe as any other date." Hailey gave her a little shove toward the door. "Go forth and hook a good one!"

"Bye," she said instead of what politeness kept her from saying—*no way in hell I'm doing this.*

"I'll follow up next time I see you!" Hailey caroled in her cheerful dictator voice.

Julia hugged her new book to her as she stepped into the bracingly cold winter air and headed around the corner to where she'd parked her car. Rejuvenation was what she needed, not blind dates. But then she remembered her goal. The whole reason she'd reached out to Hailey. She needed to find someone long enough for Angel to move on. His future happiness meant more to her than any uncomfortable nerves.

She slipped into her black Honda Civic and started the car. She gave it a minute; the old car always ran choppy on cold days. Angel was her rock, and she couldn't risk losing him as a friend. Their attraction in weak moments was something she acted on and neither one of them could control.

Julia had been a terrible wife. A terrible girlfriend too. But, dammit, she needed to be a good widow.

2

After Julia got some orgasmic relief from the firestorm Damon
had ignited, she stayed up late reading *Rejuvenate Your Life
Through Decluttering*. The next morning, New Year's Eve, she
rolled out of bed, inspired by the book to get started on the
decluttering. A New Year always made her want to do something to improve herself. Last year it had been to eat healthier,
and she'd lost twenty pounds.

She quickly showered, grabbed a piece of toast, and did a
slow tour of the small cluttered two-bedroom ranch house
she'd lived in for most of her adult life, eight years now,
trying to decide which room would give some immediate
results. She wanted to accomplish something before Angel
arrived at six to celebrate a quiet New Year's at home with
appetizers and a movie.

She stopped at the door to the master bedroom and stilled.
This was the room that still held most of Brad's things—his
half of the dresser, his nightstand, the closet. She hadn't
touched his things and wouldn't now either. She crossed back
to the living room and decided to tackle the two floor-to-
ceiling bookcases dominating one wall. They were filled to
overflowing with books, old magazines, various knickknacks
she'd collected over the years, framed pictures, and DVDs.

Everything was stacked in two rows, one in front of the other or piled on top. It was something she looked at every day, this wall of clutter. She picked up a small Statue of Liberty from when she and Brad had toured it. They'd only had a month after the wedding before he had to go to boot camp and then ship out for his mandatory three-year tour of duty with the army (he'd been ROTC in college). She couldn't throw this out, could she? Everything associated with Brad seemed sacred now. But she had to start somewhere. She'd put it in a box. She had plenty of boxes in the basement.

She headed through the kitchen and stopped short at the basement door. A chill ran through her, thinking of all the reminders of Brad down there—his boxes of stuff from his parents' house and the home gym. She whirled and started rummaging through kitchen cabinets instead. They had tons of wedding gifts they'd never opened or used, mostly appliances. Bingo! She emptied a large box that held a breadmaker. She'd donate this! A sudden lightness filled her as though some of the heavy cloak of grief slipped from one shoulder.

With renewed enthusiasm, she returned to the bookcase with the empty breadmaker box and began two piles—donate and Brad stuff. It was mostly donate. She was ruthless, wanting to see empty shelves and only her most prized possessions, like her battered copy of *Wuthering Heights*, a small collection of favorite books, and the framed pictures. She didn't need DVDs. She could always stream it. And with each item she released, a small bit of light leaked into her dark life. She opened the living room drapes for the first time in forever, the harsh sun reflecting off the snow blinding her for a moment.

She looked out to the other ranch houses on the street, built in the 1950s, and wondered what her neighbors were doing. Fieldridge, Connecticut, was a sleepy, suburban town not far from where Angel had grown up in Clover Park. Brad had bought this house as a surprise wedding gift for her, reasoning there was plenty of Angel's family nearby to look in on her while he was away. His logic at the time hadn't made sense to her. It was like Brad expected to die and expected Angel's family to take her in. Only why would they? She wasn't married to Angel. Anyway, it didn't matter because Angel never invited her to join his family for anything. Not since Brad had first died and it had been too painful for her to be alone.

Dammit. Stop thinking about Brad. She was so tired of carrying the heavy cloak of grief on her shoulders. She honored her husband's memory on the anniversary of his death every November nineteenth. She'd lived in a state of quiet remorse for years. When would she ever be able to move on?

She returned to the bookcase and stopped in front of the three framed pictures—her wedding picture, Brad in his army fatigues, and her favorite, Brad, her, and Angel on their graduation day (Brad and Angel were two years older than her), enclosing her in the safety of their arms slung over each other. She lingered on the wedding picture. She looked so young, smiling for the camera all while racked with guilt over her attraction to the best man, Angel, who she'd slept with only eight months before, and her near panic that Brad was heading out to a war zone much too soon. She'd been too young to marry, but she'd convinced herself, in her confused emotional state of guilt and worry, that marrying Brad was the right thing to do. He needed someone to come home to. A shocking surge of anger over her fucked-up life had her snatching up the picture frames, tossing them on the sofa, and then with huge sweeps, she cleared every damned shelf. Sweep, crash! Sweep, crash! Books, DVDs, shells, every piece of crap she clung to piled on the floor in a mountainous mess.

She coughed like crazy from the dust and stepped back. Wow. That felt good.

An hour later, she'd scrubbed the hell out of the wood shelves, the scent of lemon Pledge filling the air. She put only her favorite books and the picture frames back, took one look at the pile of stuff on the floor, and knew she needed more boxes. Her knees locked.

That meant the basement.

Just go!

She whirled, took a step, and nearly did a face-plant as she tripped on her own damn coffee table, slamming her shin against it. *Ouch.* She righted herself and continued through the kitchen to the basement door, her legs moving in a jerky stride, like they were frozen and it was only sheer will that had them moving. She opened the basement door, flicked on the light, and descended slowly into the dimly lit space.

She shivered at the damp and took in the piles of boxes from when they'd moved in. The movers had packed for them, and they weren't labeled other than "storage." A lot of them held Brad's childhood stuff. In the corner was a small home gym—punching bag, rowing machine, treadmill—that he'd used religiously. He needed to keep fit to be a soldier, he'd always said. She hadn't wanted him to be a soldier, but it was what he wanted, so she'd supported his decision. She snagged a couple of empty boxes and found herself frozen in place as a chill wrapped its ghostly arms around her like Brad wanted her to stay. Goosebumps broke out all over her body. She half expected to hear his voice, though it had been so long she couldn't even remember what he sounded like.

She blinked in the dim light, straining to hear him, but all she heard was the roar of her own heartbeat pounding in her ears. Suddenly the heater kicked on with a growl of machinery, and she whirled, racing back upstairs. She slammed the basement door and paced the kitchen, catching her breath.

Okay, okay, it's just your overactive imagination.

A full-body shiver ran through her, and she bolted to the living room. Music would help. She got out her phone, plugged in earbuds, and got back to work to the soothing tones of Coldplay. When she finished, she ate a quick lunch and flopped down on the beige sofa, staring at her handiwork—two clean, uncluttered bookcases with only her very favorite things. She was tired, but in a good way. One room a day was the most she could do by herself. It was too physically and emotionally draining for more. Her cell phone buzzed in her nearby purse. She retrieved it and saw a text from Hailey. She sorely regretted giving her cell number to the woman. She was like a bulldog with a pretty princess face. *Did you set up your profile?* Hailey asked.

What profile?

For eLoveMatch?

Julia bit her lip. *Not yet.*

Want me to help?

I got it.

Text me when you get it set up, and I'll help you pick matches.

Her world faded to a weird distant buzz in her ears, her mind overwhelmed and shutting down. She promptly lay down on the sofa, curled up on her side, and napped.

When she woke, she closed the curtains again, took a deep breath, and retrieved her laptop. She had to be strong for Angel's sake. She pulled up eLoveMatch, scanned it quickly for the instructions, and set up her profile. The minute she hit send, she broke into a clammy sweat, ran to the bathroom, and threw up. Damn, this moving-forward stuff sucked.

Three hours later, Julia had cleaned up and calmed herself down by snacking on crackers and getting ready for her annual New Year's Eve celebration with Angel. She cooked up some appetizers and chilled the champagne. Then she put on her favorite black polka-dot fleece pajamas.

Angel showed up right on time and politely knocked, though she'd given him a spare key years ago. He lived in the same town, only a five-minute drive away.

She opened the door, took in his familiar features—dark brown tousled hair, warm chocolate brown eyes, classically handsome Italian nose and cheekbones—and a surge of affection rushed through her. Just seeing him made her world right itself again. She wanted to throw her arms around him and hug him, but she knew she couldn't. He hadn't touched her in five years, and she would *not* be the one to cross that line again. Still she lingered, the warmth of his gaze holding her in thrall. Nothing mattered except that Angel was here.

He flashed a dimpled smile, white teeth bright against olive skin and a dark five o'clock shadow on his square jaw. "You going to let me in?"

She shook her head and laughed. "Yes! Come in." She

stepped back. He slipped past her, close enough she could breathe in his scent; leather, ocean from his cologne, and Angel. Honestly, she was shocked he hadn't found anyone yet. At thirty, he still looked young and fit with defined muscles from his workout routine. Maybe it was because he'd never been the party or club type. He'd never even touched alcohol in college, though now he had the occasional beer. He'd been their designated driver. That was Angel in a nutshell—always the good one.

He peeled off his black leather jacket, revealing a navy blue long-sleeved shirt that showed his lean, muscular frame off to perfection. She sucked in a breath. Why was she suddenly ogling her best friend? Was rejuvenating her life through decluttering waking up her libido? Her vibrator served as stress relief more than an outlet of desire for anyone. Woo! That book was dangerous.

Or maybe it was Damon in *Fierce Longing* that woke up her libido.

Either way, when Angel turned to hang his jacket on a hook by the door, she couldn't help ogling his ass too. He turned back, and she jerked her chin up, meeting his eyes. He didn't look like he'd noticed. She had to get herself under control. They were best friends. She couldn't afford to screw things up any more than they already were between them. And she definitely couldn't handle him bailing on her again.

"Happy New Year," he said.

"Happy New Year. What're we watching?"

He held up the DVD. *"The Martian That Ate Manhattan."* He loved bad B-movies, found them hysterical.

"That sounds terrible."

He grinned, and her pulse kicked up. "It got the worst rating in nineteen seventy-three."

She tore her gaze away. This was not the plan at all.

She fluttered a hand in the air. "Well, you sure can pick 'em."

He slowly walked over to the bookcases. "Wow. Julia, it looks great in here. I like the way you put the books by color and height. And all your favorites." She was a total book-worm and had been scribbling her own stories in notebooks since she could hold a pen. It was a necessity with her overactive imagination. Either that or go nuts from the chaos in her head—voices, scenes, bottled emotions—they had to come out somehow. Angel knew about her stories, though she'd never shared them with him.

She joined him, pleased he'd noticed her efforts and pretty damn proud of herself for what she'd accomplished. "It was like a little rat warren before, right?"

He turned to her, a small smile playing over his lips. "Not that bad. Just cluttered."

"I got this new book, *Rejuvenate Your Life Through Decluttering*."

He raised a brow. "And did it rejuvenate you?"

"Actually, yeah."

He stepped closer to the shelf with the three framed pictures standing alone in their place of honor. "You look so young in this wedding picture."

"I was young. Nineteen."

He stared at the picture of the three of them, carefully avoiding the solo picture of Brad. "Now you're an ancient twenty-eight."

"Hey, you'll always be older."

One corner of his mouth lifted. "True." He sniffed the air. "What'd you make? Something cheesy?"

"Cheese popovers."

"Yes!" He set the DVD on the coffee table and headed to the kitchen. "What else?"

She shuffled along behind him in her socks, careful to keep her gaze above the waist. "Mushroom caps, mozzarella sticks, and mini hot dogs."

He turned and patted his flat stomach. "Not on my healthy diet."

"It's a holiday."

He flashed a smile that lit up his face. Her breath caught. "So it is. Any New Year's resolutions?"

She brushed past him, busying herself checking on the popovers through the lit oven window. "Actually, yes."

"Well, you don't need to lose weight, so cross that one off."

She straightened. "Thanks," she said dryly, setting the timer for a couple more minutes. That had been her resolution last New Year's, and Angel had helped her by adopting the same healthy diet. She'd lost twenty pounds to his five. It had taken her ten months; him two weeks. So unfair.

Angel mumbled something.

"What?" She turned and stepped closer. He jumped back. She hadn't realized how close he'd been standing. He was so damn careful not to touch her. A constant reminder of the shameful regret they both carried. That only steeled her resolve to carry through with her plan, which meant online dating.

She took a deep breath and hesitated. Could she really go through with it? Because in setting Angel free, she'd be opening herself up to who knew what waited for her out in the real world. She'd been wrapped in her safe cocoon for so long it made her nauseous to even think about meeting a stranger for a date.

Angel pulled a kitchen chair out. "Hey, take a seat. You feeling okay?" He gestured toward the chair, and when she didn't move, he came to her side and sort of herded her over there, coming just short of touching her. He was three inches taller than her, and he used his larger body to shield and guide her without actually making contact. She complied, dropping to the seat. He went to the sink and got her a glass of water.

She took a long drink and set the glass down. He took the seat next to her and leaned close, his dark brown eyes full of kindness and concern. He was a school social worker at the same school where she taught and an excellent listener. "Better?" he asked.

She nodded. The timer on the oven dinged.

"Sit," he said. "I got it."

He pulled the potholders from the middle drawer to the left of the oven and took the popovers out. Then he slipped in the tray of mozzarella sticks she'd prepared.

"Four twenty-five," she told him. He adjusted the temperature and helped himself to a beer from the fridge. She kept his favorite kind on hand. She watched as he pulled the bottle opener from the third drawer on the right. His familiarity with the kitchen made her realize she and Angel were like an old married couple minus the sex. She'd let this go on long enough. Angel deserved so much better.

He remained standing, taking a sip of beer and watching her over the rim. "What is it?"

She clasped her hands tightly together, suddenly nervous that Angel would fight her on this. He'd been so protective of her since Brad died. "I, uh, I signed up for an online dating site."

His jaw dropped, and the beer slipped from his hand, hitting the old linoleum floor with a thud and then a bounce. Beer spewed everywhere. She leaped up, grabbed some paper towels and hurried over to clean the mess. Angel stood frozen in place, saying nothing. It scared the hell out of her. She'd never seen him shocked into speechlessness.

She sopped up what she could—it was nearly a full bottle —and tossed the towels and bottle in the trash. Then she grabbed more paper towels, the kitchen still eerily silent. "Angel? Please say something."

Still nothing.

She glanced over, took in his clenched jaw, his lips a flat line, and swallowed hard. He remained silent as she knelt at his feet and cleaned up the rest of the wet floor. She yelped as he suddenly grabbed her by the upper arms and yanked her to her feet. Not only because he hadn't touched her in five years, and his fingers were burning through the thin fleece, it was his grip, tight and unforgiving. Her fingers clenched the sopping wet paper towels, beer dripping between them, soaking the floor, soaking her socks.

"Let me throw these out," she said, her voice unnaturally high. Angel never lost his temper with her. With Brad, yes, but never her.

He gave her a little shake, and she squeaked. "You're ready to date?" he asked through clenched teeth.

She sucked in a breath. No, absolutely not, but she needed to make things right. To set him free. "I-I want to try."

He leaned close, and she dropped the towels, her heart thudding against her ribcage. Angel close up overwhelmed her senses every time, but the fierce look in his eyes lit a dark desire that filled her with shame.

"With a stranger?" he bit out. "Some random asshole you met over the Internet?"

She looked away. "There's nice people online too."

He released his grip on her arms and crossed to the far side of the kitchen away from her.

"It's for the best," she said, her voice shaky. "I…" She trailed off at his hard, furious look. This was not the Angel she knew. Her Angel was kind, good, unbearably sweet and tender always. Except for those times when she'd crossed the line. Then they'd both been animals, consumed by base desire heightened by the forbidden.

He advanced on her, and she braced herself. *Stay strong. For once in your life, do the right thing with Angel.* He stopped short a foot away. "No. I won't allow it."

She bristled at his authoritative tone. "You're not. .you don't get a say."

"The hell I don't."

"Best friends are supposed to—"

He grabbed her and hauled her close, her softness pressed against his hard planes, filling her with traitorous heat. He'd never touched her first. It was always her.

"Please don't," she said on a near sob, turning her head away. This wasn't going to help either of them. One kiss and they'd be naked. It was out of control. But Angel and sex had always been wrong. Always been her weak spot. Brad had no idea the kind of wife she'd been. The kind of girlfriend. But it was even worse now. With their twisted history, she and Angel couldn't…she felt light-headed. He'd bail for good this time. Just the thought of losing Angel forever robbed her breath.

"Julia." The one word was a harsh demand and rasp of frustration at the same time. "Look at me."

"Please," she whispered. "You're the only person I can count on. The only thing that kept me sane when the grief was too much." She licked her dry lips. "You deserve…" She trailed off as he leaned close, her mind suddenly blank.

"What do I deserve?" he asked, his voice a husky rumble in her ear.

"We never should've been together," she blurted. The words flew from her mouth before she could soften them.

He pulled away. The loss of him, his heat, his rock-steady body, nearly made her weep.

He rubbed the back of his neck and avoided her eyes. Her stomach turned. She hadn't meant to hurt him. "Angel, I'm so sorry."

He looked toward the door. "I should go."

"Please don't. New Year's won't be the same without you." They'd shared ten years' worth of New Year's Eves together. Sometimes with other people, but always together.

A muscle ticked in his jaw, his eyes still on the door. Time was running out to fix things between them tonight. She feared time was running out to fix things between them period.

"Can't we have a do-over?" she asked desperately. They'd had a few of those already—Angel's idea—when they needed to…reestablish the boundaries of their relationship.

He jabbed a finger at her. "You don't want me? Fine! But Internet dating is a mistake. You don't know who's going to show up at your door."

She'd always wanted him. That wasn't the problem. The problem was their friendship couldn't take another wild night that ended in shame and regret. The last time, after Brad's funeral…she thought she'd die from the cool distance Angel kept. It had taken months for anything close to their old friendship to return. And the careful way he kept his distance ever since then, jumping back at the slightest chance of contact, was a sharp reminder of not only what they'd done, but what they'd lost as friends. No more easy affection, no teasing banter, no hugs after a rough day. Nothing.

She sucked in a breath. "It's just—"

"Fuck it. I don't want to hear it." He stormed out of the kitchen. A moment later, the front door slammed behind him.

She winced. She should've handled that better. Explained herself better.

Dammit. Why couldn't she find a way for both of them to move forward?

3

Ten years ago...

Angel had never believed in love at first sight until the day he met Julia MacKendrick. It was the first week of a new school year at college, and she'd been sitting alone in the lounge of the coed honors dorm where he lived—reserved for students there on academic scholarship—her nose in a book. Her hair was dark brown, softly sweeping past her angular face with its high cheekbones and cute pointed chin, and trailing to just past her shoulders. She sat cross-legged, oblivious to the noisy chatter of another group of students across the room. He instantly knew two things—she was shy; he had to meet her.

He stopped in front of her, took a quick look at her book, and came up with the best line he could think of, one book-worm to another. "Good book."

Her head snapped up, her dark blue eyes widening in surprise, her skin a creamy white like the porcelain doll his stepmom had, her cheeks a rosy pink. She took his breath away. Then she spoke, her voice soft and uncertain, drawing out a protective instinct he didn't even know he had. "You like *Wuthering Heights*?"

He cleared his throat. He didn't want to start things with a lie; he'd never actually read it. The cover had a woman on it from a long-ago time, like an old painting. "I heard good things. You new here? A freshman?"

The noisy group left and rushed out the door. It was close to dinnertime. People were heading to the cafeteria.

She tucked a lock of hair behind her ear. "Yeah."

"I'm a junior. I could show you around." He held out his hand. "Angel Marino."

She shook his hand in a weak grip, the touch sparking between them. She met his eyes with a light of surprise before pulling her hand back. She'd felt it too. "Julia MacKendrick."

"Nice to meet you, Julia."

"You too." She tucked her bookmark into her book. "I found my way around campus okay," she quickly added.

He jerked his thumb toward the door. "I'm meeting my friend for dinner. You want to come?"

She gripped her book tightly in her hands. "I wouldn't want to intrude."

He sensed she wanted to go, but was nervous. After all, he was an upperclassman and she didn't know him. But she would.

"Not at all." He offered her his arm, bending it at the elbow and leaning close.

She stood, just a few inches shorter than his own five foot ten, and their gazes locked. A long electric moment passed, a connection of one soul to another, before she turned away and tucked her book in her purse. "Okay, my roommate ate earlier, so…" She trailed off and headed toward the door.

He rushed ahead and held the door open for her. They stepped out into the crisp sunshine of September in Connecticut. The trees were just starting to turn, bright yellow bursting among the green, the sky bright blue, the clouds white and fluffy. A perfect fall day. He led the way to the cafeteria, racking his brain for stuff to say that would naturally lead to asking her out. He'd never been as smooth with girls as his older brothers, so he finally blurted, "Tell me about you."

"Oh—" she laughed "—really not much to tell."

"What's your major?"

"Elementary Education. I want to be a teacher." He loved that. She liked kids. So did he.

"I'm thinking about being a family social worker," he told her.

"That's really important work," she said.

"Or a psychologist," he added. "I haven't decided. People say I'm a good listener."

She studied him for a moment. "I could see that about you."

By the time they'd gotten their food—and he'd spent entirely too much time breathing in her fruity shampoo—he was so deep in lust he was having trouble speaking coherently. They found an empty table in the corner. His best friend, Brad Turner, was late as usual. The big goofball. They'd met freshman year in Psych 101 when Brad had slipped him a drawing of the professor—a distinguished older gentleman—riding a donkey, naked. Brad cracked him up and reminded him of his stepbrother Jared, who'd gone to college out of state. Poor Brad had to take summer classes to keep from flunking out and was on academic probation.

Angel kept up a steady stream of questions, both because he wanted to know her and because he was working up the nerve to ask her out. She gradually relaxed, telling him about her favorite books and TV shows, meeting his eyes more. This filled him with pride, his ability to make anyone comfortable in a conversation.

"What about your family?" he asked. "Any brothers or sisters?" He came from a large close-knit family of his dad, stepmom, two biological brothers, and three stepbrothers. He was the youngest. He hoped family was important to her too.

She tucked her hair behind both ears. "No, actually, my mom couldn't have kids."

"Oh. So…" Did she mean ever? Or after she had Julia?

She stared at the table. "I'm adopted."

"Oh. How is that? Do you like your adoptive parents? I mean, of course you do. Sorry."

She met his eyes with a weak smile. "It's okay. I'm actually still getting used to it. I just found out when I turned eighteen in June."

"Three months ago?"

She nodded.

"That must've been a shock."

"It was." Her blue eyes flashed. "I'm still pissed at them. That was a hell of a bombshell to drop on my graduation day. Congratulations! You're not one of us, and there's no more where you came from." She bit her lip. "My biological mother died years before. No one told me shit." She gave him a watery smile, and his chest clutched. "I'm not who I thought I was."

"But you're still you. Just with a new perspective."

She shook her head. "You don't understand."

"You're right, but I'm a good listener. You want to go somewhere to talk?"

She looked at him for a long moment, taking his measure, he supposed. "Where?"

"There's a pond out behind the agricultural building."

"You're not…dangerous, are you?"

"Smart girl." He smiled, knowing his dimpled smile made him look as angelic as his nickname, Angel, short for Angelo. "I'm harmless, I promise."

She studied him again, and he worked hard to hide the lust that only increased the more time they spent together. "Okay," she said. "You have a trustworthy face."

He stood, quietly victorious. "I do, don't I? Let's go."

They talked for hours, sitting on the grassy hill by the pond, mostly Julia, who was still coming to terms with being adopted and grappling with anger and grief over her biological mother, who'd died when she was eight. His own biological mother had died when he was five, but he kept that to himself because this was about her and her feelings. He'd learned all about the importance of validating feelings in his advanced psych course. Julia broke down in tears, and he sat in silent companionship, aching to hold her, yet knowing it was too soon. Finally she quieted.

"Sorry," she said in a small voice. "I guess I didn't realize how much it still bothered me."

"It's still very new for you." Now he couldn't ask her out. She was too upset.

She swatted her arm. "The mosquitoes are coming out. We should get back."

He stood and walked her back to the dorm. Brad was in the lounge, playing foosball with Mike, probably waiting for him. Brad caught sight of him, took in Julia with an appreciative look, and bounded over to them. Angel was instantly wary. Brad with his golden looks and big personality easily eclipsed Angel whenever they met a group of girls, hogging all of the attention. This was one girl he didn't want Brad taking an interest in.

"You stood me up, you jerk!" Brad punched Angel's arm. "I couldn't find you in the caf."

"You were late," Angel said.

"I was raised by mules," Brad quipped. "Bunch of asses." He winked at Julia. "Adopted, of course."

"I was adopted," Julia said quietly.

"Oh." Brad turned uncharacteristically serious. "Uh, me too. It's a bit of a *fuck you* to have your real mom hand you over, ain't it?" Was Brad adopted? He'd never mentioned it before.

Julia brightened. "The biggest *fuck you* there is."

Brad grinned and moved in closer to Julia, making her cheeks flush bright pink. "You want to get wasted?"

Angel's protective instinct kicked in hard. "Brad, this is her first week. She's a freshman."

Brad shot him a dark look. "Quiet, choirboy."

"Yes," Julia said.

Brad grinned. "C'mon. I've got a six-pack in my room. It's across campus. I'm not honors material." Brad bounded out the door, heading toward his dorm. Julia ran after him, and Angel followed to make sure she stayed safe.

Later, Angel walked a drunk Julia back to her room, untouched by either of them. Brad had passed out on his bed after chugging four beers in rapid succession. Julia had two, and Angel abstained so he could keep an eye on her. She was a cheerful drunk and babbled happily about her two new best friends—him and Brad. He saw her safely inside her room and went to his room, knowing he had to stake his claim where Julia was concerned. He didn't have the appeal of Brad, but he felt deep down that he and Julia were two parts of a whole. Just being near her made him feel amazing. Imagine if he actually got to touch her.

The next day he stopped by Brad's room at noon, their normal time to meet up for lunch on Saturday.

He took one look at his best friend and blurted, "I saw Julia first."

Brad said nothing, which was unusual for him, just put his video game controller down and got off the bed, shoving his feet into sneakers.

"I'm asking her out," Angel said.

Brad looked at him, more serious than he'd ever been in the two years he'd known him. "We'll let Julia decide who she wants."

A rare temper flared. "No. Back off." Angel shoved Brad, who was an inch shorter but strong and stocky.

Brad shoved Angel back. "You back off."

"I saw her first!"

"She's not a damn toy. She's a person."

"You're just going to use her! Find someone else to hook up with." Brad was notorious for hooking up and then dumping the girl.

Brad stormed past him and into the hallway, striding toward the stairs.

Angel followed. "Where are you going?"

"To Julia's room." Julia had told them her room number in her drunken state and invited them to stop by any time to hang out.

They marched straight out of Brad's dorm and over to the honors dorm in furious silence. Brad reached her door first and knocked.

Julia answered, her long dark brown hair falling in a

gentle wave over her shoulders, her dark blue eyes looking curiously from Brad to Angel. "Hey, guys, what's up?"

Angel was momentarily speechless as his emotions tangled up with awe at her beauty. His heart was pounding in his ears.

Brad spoke up. "Two strays like us should party—"

"Are you adopted?" Angel asked Brad.

Brad ignored him. "Up for it tonight? I'll pick you up at nine."

Julia looked to Angel. "Will you be there?"

His heart filled with hope. "Yeah."

"Great!" She turned to her roommate, a pretty blond girl in tight jeans. More Brad's usual type. "Mandy, we're going to a party."

"Awesome," Mandy said.

"See ya tonight," Brad said. Then he grabbed Julia and kissed her deeply; his tongue must've been halfway down her throat. Angel was about to yank Brad away when Julia's arms wrapped around Brad's neck. Angel stepped back.

Julia looked dazed when Brad released her, her fingers resting on her lips. From that moment on, Julia only had eyes for Brad.

Angel hated Brad with every fiber of his being. Their friendship ended immediately.

Yet, four months later, Brad went to Angel's room and apologized. He said he was serious about Julia and had even joined Army ROTC in an effort to be the man Julia deserved. Angel could see the change in his former friend—his seriousness, his drive to do better, his good grades, and, after Brad confided he planned on proposing to Julia on graduation day, Angel knew whatever claim he'd had on Julia was gone forever. He forgave Brad.

The three of them became inseparable. Always Julia, Brad, and Angel. He and Brad picked up where they left off. He and Julia got to know each other as friends and became very, very close. Julia turned to Angel whenever she needed to talk, whenever there was an issue with Brad; whenever or whatever way she needed him, he was there. And the moment

Brad was out of the picture, back home in September of their senior year with a bad case of mono, Angel and Julia gave in to the attraction they'd both done their best to ignore.

It was wrong and so right and hot as all hell.

That weekend lived long in his memory. It had to.

Until the next time.

4

———

Julia's stomach was in knots and her hands shook slightly, but she was determined to go through with this blind date. Someone, Anthony, had responded to her profile with a request to meet for coffee. It had only been two days since she'd joined the dating website, but she figured there were a lot of single people out there determined to change their single status in the New Year. She hadn't had a date in so long she wasn't even sure she knew what to do.

Angel had stopped by yesterday, New Year's Day, and invited her to visit the sick kids in the cancer ward with his brothers. She took that as a peace offering and happily joined him. Besides, she wanted to get more involved in the community. She spent too much time in her own head. On the ride over, Angel had asked about the online dating site, his tone more curious than angry, so she'd told him about her dopey profile with her teacher picture and her made-up interests—cooking and hiking. She'd thought it sounded better than the truth, and she wanted to attract the kind of man interested in a woman like that. Angel made her promise to tell him where and when she'd be meeting someone and to call him if she felt uncomfortable for any reason.

She took a deep breath and set about picking an outfit, finally settling on a simple dark blue V-neck sweater that matched her eyes, with a black pencil skirt and knee-high black leather boots. She hoped the outfit said casual, hip, and with-it. Though she was the farthest thing from it. She applied makeup and gave herself a silent pep talk. *This doesn't have to be a big deal. Just a baby step.*

She grabbed her cell, desperately wanting to hear Angel's voice. He always calmed her down when she got worked up, but she knew she had to stop running to him with every single problem in her life. She played his last message to her, needing to hear the deep, familiar baritone of his voice. "Hey, Julia, call me when you get back from your date." There was a long pause. "I'm proud of you. Okay, bye."

Tears sprang to her eyes. He wouldn't be proud if he knew what a wreck she was. Maybe she should cancel. She still had an hour before she had to leave.

The doorbell rang. Shit! Her heart raced. What should she do?

She stepped out to the living room and stared at the door. Wait. She was supposed to meet her date at the café. Anthony didn't know her address.

She peeked through the peephole. Nobody was there. Maybe she had a delivery. She opened the door and looked down. No package. A ping rang out against the gutter on the side of the house. She looked up, was it hailing? Suddenly she was blindfolded, a soft cloth covered her eyes and wrapped around her head from behind. She screamed and a hand covered her mouth. She fought her attacker, elbowing them in the gut, and was pulled tight against a hard male chest.

"Shh, it's me," he said in her ear.

Angel! She stopped struggling, but her heart still raced, morphing from fear to excitement as she remembered Damon from *Fierce Longing* and how he'd grabbed Mia from behind, his hand over her mouth, before taking her to his estate and having his wicked, wicked way with her.

He turned her to face him, his hands restraining her arms at her sides, preventing her from pulling off the blindfold.

Her pulse pounded in her ears. "What the hell are you doing? You scared me!"

He kept a tight hold on her, and her mind flashed to the dining room table where Damon seduced Mia into an open surrender. "My name is Angelo, and I'm your blind date."

A laugh bubbled up inside her. "Is that why you blindfolded me? I don't think this is how blind dates work."

"I'm someone new you're meeting, and we're having our first date." She could hear the smile in his voice and found herself smiling back.

They'd never had an actual date. Two hookups, one almost hookup that Angel stopped, and ten years of friendship, but no date.

"What about my actual date?" she asked.

"I left word at the café that you had to cancel permanently."

"Angel!" She struggled to lift her arms to take off the blindfold, but he was stronger and determined.

"Leave it. And answer me honestly, did you really want to meet this guy, or were you dreading it?"

She pressed her lips together, not wanting to admit the truth. He knew her too well.

"I thought so," he gloated. "Wait here while I get your coat and purse, and no peeking."

She heard the front door open, and then a few moments later, he was back, locking up for her. He helped her on with her coat and put the purse strap over her shoulder. A frisson of excitement ran through her. He held her by the elbow, his other hand on her lower back as he guided her down the front porch steps and to his car.

"Where are we going?" she asked.

"Someplace special."

She heard the door creak open on his Honda Civic. They'd bought identical cars together, years ago, to get a better deal. He guided her in, his hand on her head to prevent her from bumping it. His scent lingered in the car, heightened by the blindfold, a little bit of his cologne—ocean and subtle spice— a lot of Angel.

Once he got in and started the car, she spoke up. "Do you know why I signed up for online dating?"

"Yeah, because you're ready to date." He backed out of the driveway and turned on to the main road. "You warm enough?" He cranked the heat, but it took forever in the old car to really get warm.

"I'm fine. Angel, I...please don't take this the wrong way—"

"It's Angelo and, whatever reason you signed up for that dating site, I don't care. You wanted to meet someone new, and tonight you're meeting someone new."

"But I know it's you. Can I please take off the blindfold?"

"No. That's part of the surprise."

She found herself smiling. "Is it Burger Shack?" They often went there for special occasions. Neither of them had a lot of money. She'd donated the money she'd received on Brad's death to the Wounded Veterans Alliance to help other soldiers get back on their feet. She hadn't wanted to benefit from his death. Not after she'd wronged him.

"Does that sound like a surprise?" Angel asked. "No, someplace fancy like you deserve."

"Angel," she said softly. She didn't want him spending a lot of money on her.

"Angelo," he corrected.

"Angelo—" the name felt foreign and new on her tongue "—you can't afford that."

"I have money stashed away."

"For your house!" He'd been saving for a house for years.

"This is more important. You're more important."

She got quiet. The last thing she wanted was to hurt her best friend. But wasn't this date just leading him on?

"Ang—"

"Say the whole name or I'm not answering."

She bristled at his bossy tone. "Angelo," she said tightly, "I'm not sure what you think this...date is, but—"

"What did you think your blind date would be today?"

"Horrible," she admitted.

He barked out a laugh. "I knew it. You want to know what tonight is? This is our do-over. Big time. We just met. I think you're the most beautiful woman I've ever clapped eyes on, and I'm dying to touch you." He took her hand, his larger hand enveloping hers in warmth, the firm clasp immediately relaxing her. She'd so missed his touch, even if it was wrong to crave it.

"You're so forward, Angelo. We just met."

He chuckled. "I'll be a perfect gentleman, I promise."

"Do you ever regret—"

"I regret nothing," he said fiercely. "Not one thing I've ever done." He paused and then continued in a more relaxed tone. "Tell me what you do for fun."

"I enjoy cooking and hiking and sunsets."

He laughed. "Me too. I'm also in a motorcycle club."

"I knew that the minute I saw your black leather jacket."

"Did you peek? Because I believe you've been blindfolded for this entire blind date."

She reached over to feel the sleeve of his familiar leather jacket and met with the soft feel of a suit jacket. "How fancy is this place?"

"You'll see."

She shook her head, smiling. This was so much better than the ordeal she'd thought she'd be going through tonight, but still…was it right? She leaned her head back on the headrest, letting herself imagine for a moment that she was on a first date with a man named Angelo. That he was taking her some-place special. That he thought she was beautiful. And he was funny and kind and smelled wonderful. What would she do in that situation? For just a little while, she wanted to pretend, to enjoy what he was offering.

"Where are you from, Angelo?"

"I'm from Clover Park, Connecticut, raised by two loving parents, five older brothers who had my back, and a commu-nity of people who really cared. How about you?"

"I was adopted by two loving parents and always wished for a sister." Angel had helped her come to terms with being adopted, further helped along by Brad also being adopted. The shared sense of abandonment over being given up by their mothers was what bonded her and Brad tightly together. His situation had been far worse, stuck in an orphanage until he was five, then a series of foster homes before he was finally adopted at ten by a strict couple he couldn't seem to please. Though he tried his best to make them glad they adopted him, they were never close. Brad told her never to bring up his adoption issues to her parents or his; it was a touchy subject and something he only wanted to share with her. She agreed, deeply touched that he'd confided his painful past to her. It wasn't difficult to keep his confidence since neither of them were close to their parents. She'd since made amends with her parents, though the sense of abandonment never left her. It made her cling tighter to what she had, which made Brad's death even more difficult.

"My husband was adopted too," she added. She held her breath, wondering if she was allowed to bring up Brad. She would if she really was on a first date, especially since her profile said she was a widow. She'd been prepared to discuss it.

There was a long silence.

"Forget I said that," she blurted.

"I'm glad you both found your forever families. I remember your profile said you were a widow. Can I ask what happened to your husband?"

"He died a hero, throwing himself on an explosive device to save his unit." She'd rehearsed that line so she could say it smoothly. It was the truth, but she still found it hard to say. She'd had nightmares about it for years. Her husband was a hero, and she'd betrayed him. The heavy guilt weighed on her, making it hard to breathe.

Angel broke into her dark thoughts. "Take a breath."

She did, trying not to think about how well he knew her, knew her frailties, and accepted them.

"I'm sorry to hear about your husband," he said. "How long has it been?"

"Five years."

"And are you ready for a new relationship?"

The question hung in the air. Was she ready? Her whole single life had been wrapped up in Brad. He'd been her first kiss, her first lover, her first everything. How crazy was that?

She was twenty-eight and this was only her second "new" date her entire life.

"You don't have to answer that," Angel said. "Let's just see how tonight goes. No pressure. You like cats? I have three."

She burst out laughing. He didn't. But he sure could get creative. "I love cats. I have ten."

"Ten, huh? We should have a cat party. Catnip, feather toys, the whole deal."

"My cats would love that."

"How you like living in Fieldridge?"

"It's okay."

Angel, playing the part of Angelo to the fullest, kept up a steady stream of small talk she imagined people had when they went on a first date. She'd spent her first date with Brad drunk at a party in someone's off-campus apartment.

A short while later, they arrived at a restaurant with soft music playing and low conversation. She hoped she wasn't underdressed. Angel spoke quietly to someone and then guided her to her seat, one hand on her lower back. He removed her blindfold while standing behind her. She blinked, adjusting to the light, and took in a fancy French restaurant with white tablecloths and too much silverware.

"Oh," she breathed. "It's so nice."

He sat across from her, and she burst out laughing.

"What?" He bit back a smile, his dimples showing in his clean-shaven cheeks. He wore a thick fake mustache that curled up at the ends.

"Take it off," she gasped through her laughter.

He cocked his head quizzically. "Take what off?"

She couldn't stop laughing.

"What? I needed a disguise so it feels fresh. You just met Angelo. Hey, it's not polite to laugh at your blind date."

She tried to restrain herself. He looked like he just got back from a disco. "Where's my disguise?"

He held up a finger and reached under the table. Then he held out black-rimmed glasses with clear lenses and handed them to her. She wore contacts to avoid glasses like this, part of her awkward, nerdy high school years.

"Put 'em on," he insisted.

"What else are you hiding under the table?"

"Never you mind. Put them on."

She slid the glasses on. "How do I look?"

He flashed a devilish smile. "Nerdy."

She huffed. "You look like a porn star from the seventies."

He crossed his arms. "That's exactly what I was going for."

She giggled. "You're something else, Angelo."

He leared across the table, his dark eyes sparkling with mischief. "So are you, Julie."

"Julia."

He straightened. "Ah, sorry. Still getting used to the name. Julia." He gave her a warm smile, and her gaze locked with his in a bond she never wanted broken. Her throat got tight. No amount of pretending could change the fact that their friendship needed to stay exactly that.

He picked up the menu and looked at her over it. "What do you think porn stars eat?"

"Oysters?"

"I'm thinking steak. A nice, *juicy* steak." He snapped his teeth at her.

She flushed and picked up her menu.

"Get whatever you want, Jill."

"Thank you, Andrew."

They cracked up, and the tension dissipated. They had a good time, trying each other's meals, sharing a dessert. She felt a lightness and easiness between them that she hadn't felt in a long time.

When they got back to her place, Angelo walked her to the door. She suddenly got nervous. If he kissed her, she'd cave. She knew it. She didn't want to go down that shameful path again after the good time they'd had. And she knew it would be the death knell for their friendship.

She held out her hand to shake. "Thank you for a lovely dinner, Angelo."

He took her hand, raised it to his lips, and kissed the back of it, his fake mustache tickling her fingers, his lips like warm velvet. "My pleasure, Julia." The silky words left her brain fuzzy. She could do nothing but stand there and stare.

Then he turned and left.

She went inside on shaky legs and quietly shut the door. She peeked out the living room curtains to watch him go, catching Angel doing a fist pump before he strode back to his car, got in, and drove away. She walked like a zombie to the sofa and flopped down.

What the hell just happened?

5

———

Angel missed Sunday family dinner for the first time in years for his date with Julia, and he didn't give it a second thought until his stepbrother Jared texted him later that night. *Where were you tonight?*

He hadn't wanted to tell anyone about his plan to be with Julia. The situation was too delicate, and his family was not known for their subtlety. He texted back, *I told Mom I wasn't feeling well. Didn't she tell you?*

You think I believe that bullshit excuse? You hungover?

No.

Save me some time and tell me what's up. Emily's giving me the look.

Angel chuckled. Emily was his stepbrother's fiancée, a nurse at the same hospital where Jared worked as an orthopedic surgeon. If anything, Jared was the one hounding her as soon as they got home from Sunday dinner, not the other way around. His brother was a total horndog. Hell, they all were, every one of his brothers. Him too, though he had more control. Usually. All bets were off when he got the signal from Julia. He'd tucked a condom in his wallet the moment he decided to be her blind date. Now that he'd crossed the no-touch zone, things could go from zero to explosive at any moment.

Go give her what she wants, Angel texted.

I will. Don't worry. You meet someone?

He hesitated.

Spill it.

Yes. He hated to lie. On the other hand, Jared could be relentless in his teasing and would blab within minutes to the family grapevine.

Who? Was it Julia?

Angel sucked in a breath, on shaky ground between honesty and total disaster. *How could I meet her? I already know her.* Semantics, whatever.

Name, please.

He didn't reply. His cell rang a moment later. Jared. "I'm missing out on some fine Emily action over here—"

"Jared!" Emily hollered in the background. "I'm just watching TV!"

Angel laughed.

"Don't listen to her," Jared said. "The woman is hot for me. More than anyone she's ever met in her life, right, Em?"

"No doubt," Emily replied with a laugh.

He shook his head. Angel had dated Emily a year ago, and Jared was still trying to deal with the fact that Emily had slept with Angel first. Angel had dated off and on since meeting Julia way back when, but no one ever stuck because of the hold Julia had on his heart. A painful fact. He ended things with Emily after four months, the longest he'd dated anyone, because even though she was great, a pretty pediatric nurse with a soft spot for kids, he knew he could never love her the way he loved Julia. Not that he'd ever told Julia he loved her. At first he couldn't because she was with Brad. And then she was grappling with grief and wasn't ready to hear it. Maybe this new beginning between them—

"Did you nail her?" Jared asked.

Angel scrubbed a hand over his face. "Geez, Jare. I had a first date, okay? Not everyone rushes into bed."

"You like her? More than…" His brother was showing an uncommon sensitivity by not saying Julia's name. In a text, yes, but he'd pulled back in deference to the touchy situation.

It seemed Jared falling hard for Emily had softened him a bit. But today Angel didn't mind hearing her name. Not at all.

"Yes, I liked her more than ol' Julia." New Julia was much better than old Julia.

"Well, hell, that's great news, bro. Keep me posted. Gotta go, the woman is doing a striptease."

"I am not!" Emily hollered.

"Get to it, woman," Jared said. "Bye." He hung up.

Angel stared at his phone, wanting to call Julia to check in, but something stopped him. If he really wanted to pretend they had a first date, a fresh start, he wouldn't call right away. He'd wait a day, maybe two, before following up.

Could he really start again with Julia?

God, he hoped so. He didn't think he could live in this eternal state of want for much longer. Something had to give.

Julia paced her living room, adrenaline pumping through her veins. She didn't quite know what to do with herself. Just a simple kiss on the hand, Angel's silky tone, filled her with dangerous pleasure. Angel and sex had always been wrong.

A memory of the first time she'd been with Angel came back to her in a flash so vivid she had to sit down. Brad hadn't made it back to campus at the start of his senior year because he was too sick with mono. Ironically, she was the one who gave it to him (she'd been sick most of the summer). It was the first weekend back on campus, and she'd missed Angel something fierce. He'd been working all summer, and between that and her being sick, she hadn't connected with him. But now she had him all to herself, and Brad was back home, recovering at his parents' house.

She invited Angel back to her room, knowing her roommate was away. And though he joined her there, he didn't make a move. Instead they talked all night, getting deep into philosophical discussions like why are we here on this earth? What is our purpose? What is the meaning of life? As it got late, neither one of them wanted to break the connection, this meeting of the minds that satisfied them both on a deep level. She'd changed into a T-shirt and sweats, he kept his T-shirt and jeans on, and they'd gotten comfortable, lounging on her bed as they talked into the wee hours of the night. Eventually they lay down on their sides, facing each other, talking and talking and talking. Angel's head eclipsed most of the light from her nightstand, giving him an aura that she thought almost like a halo. Her Angel, always so good to her. Unlike Brad, who sometimes made her cry with his insensitive remarks tossed out in a joking way that still managed to cut deep in her sensitive heart.

At some point Angel must've turned out the light because the next thing she knew, it was morning, the first rays of light filtering through the thin curtains, slowly making her aware of Angel spooning her from behind, one arm wrapped around her. They were on top of the covers like they'd talked until they conked out. She slowly turned to face him. He was sound asleep. She gazed at him, pretending for a moment that it was just the two of them in the world. She listened to him breathe, so steady and reassuring, like the man himself. His dark brown hair was adorably rumpled, the five o'clock shadow on his jaw more pronounced, his dark lashes sweeping over his cheeks. She let her gaze trail lower. He'd taken off his jeans and wore only a T-shirt and navy blue boxer briefs. His olive skin glowed with good health, his muscles defined from his biceps to his flat stomach to his legs, hard male perfection. Her fingers tingled, longing to touch. She forgot herself, forgot she was supposed to marry Brad at the end of the school year. Though Brad hadn't yet proposed, it was understood. She reached out to gently stroke his thick, wavy hair. She slid her fingers through it and around to the soft wave at the nape of his neck that she'd always longed to feel. His hair was so thick yet so soft.

She stroked his hair again while she looked her fill at his gorgeous face. His eyes opened suddenly, the heat in them registering on a deep primal level. Desire flooded her, making her light-headed, all of her nerve endings tingling, craving his touch. Acting on pure instinct, she cupped the back of his neck and pulled him in, placing a soft kiss on his warm lips. A jolt ran through her at the contact, their very first kiss, and her eyes met his in equal parts shock and wonder.

"Julia," he said gruffly. That one word a warning—danger ahead. Only wrapped in the cocoon of dim morning light, nothing felt more right than what she did next, showing him what she wanted because she couldn't say the words. She sat up and pulled her T-shirt over her head.

He sat up too, gazing at her for a long heated moment before he took his own T-shirt off in one quick move. She took him in hungrily, from his broad shoulders to his beautiful chest with dark hair tapering down to boxer briefs tented with a massive erection. He groaned, and then, finally he touched her, his fingers tangling in her hair as his mouth claimed hers in a hard kiss of possession. A raw, carnal need consumed her. She pressed closer, her hands frantic to touch all of him, needing to join together. A frustrated whimper of need escaped from the back of her throat as she pulled at his briefs. He pulled them off, and then he was on her, his mouth demanding, his hands rough and all over her, the fire between them out of control as they fell back on the mattress, their mouths fused together. He pulled back just long enough to yank her sweats and panties down and off before thrusting inside her. She threw her head back in exultation. He thrust deep, over and over, both of them panting, her nails scratching down his back as the pressure built, bringing her to a trembling state like she'd never experienced before, like she was about to shatter. Her eyes flew open in shock and euphoria, meeting Angel's dark heated gaze in a body and soul connection she couldn't fight, merely got sucked under, lost in it, lost in him as they raced together to what they both craved. Her climax hit in a sharp and sudden peak, the room dimming around her, and then she flew, soaring with a rush of pleasure. The room came back into focus as Angel pumped into her, rocking her with aftershocks until he exploded inside her. He stayed buried deep, his harsh breath rasping near her ear.

Slowly, reality crept in—Angel, heavy on top of her, sticky

between the legs from the wrong man, still shaky from a heart-pounding release. She took in his dark hair so different from Brad's golden blond. *The wrong man,* her brain shouted. An overwhelming remorse and guilt seized her, making it hard to breathe. She pushed him as hard as she could, both hands on his shoulders. He rolled off her, but he didn't leave. Instead he held her, side by side, chest to chest, his hand stroking her hair and down her back, soothing her. She breathed easy again, closing her eyes, lulled by the gentle strokes. A long time passed like that. Her heart resumed its steady beat, her limbs became heavy, her body melted into his heat.

"Julia," he finally said, "please tell me you're on the pill." Neither of them had thought of birth control in their desperate need.

"I am." Guilt pricked at her again, making her tense up. She was on the pill because she was in a serious relationship with Brad. She swallowed over the lump in her throat. What had she done? "You should go."

"I should, but I'm not."

"This was wrong," she whispered. "We can never do this again."

Angel kissed her fiercely, roughly, stealing her breath. She lost herself, overwhelmed with all that he made her feel. He pulled back a long moment later and spoke, the words a hot whisper against her tender lips. "What we have is right and good."

"It's wrong!" she cried.

His mouth settled over hers, softer this time, molding her to him as he cupped the back of her head. His tongue swept inside, drawing a needy whimper from the back of her throat. He deepened the kiss as his hand slid down her back, palming her ass and pressing her against his hardness. Her body drenched with throbbing need, an overwhelming craving made her rock her hips restlessly against him even as her brain screamed at her to stop the madness. She'd never craved Brad like this, once had been enough with him. It must be because Angel was forbidden. Her best friend. Brad's best friend. Angel shifted to the side of her neck, nipping and soothing with his tongue, his rough stubble scraping against her. She forced her eyes open and tried to think. Only one thing was clear—Brad was sick in bed and she screwed his best friend. Worse, she wanted to do it again. Desperately.

She rolled away from Angel, giving him her back, and he pressed close, holding her from behind. Not demanding, not pushing for anything, just holding her, bringing her comfort. She didn't know how long he held her. Her body relaxed so deeply she floated in and out of consciousness, lulled from his heat, safe in his arms where the outside world couldn't touch them. She breathed in his scent, Angel mixed with musky sex, both a potent aphrodisiac and a reminder of what they'd done wrong. Slowly, she became aware of his hardness pressing into her hip, his hand now splayed low across her belly, making her ache with desire. She told herself to pull away, but her sinner body had other ideas. She lifted her leg and wrapped it back over his, silently telling him what she wanted. He didn't hesitate, thrusting fully and deeply in one stroke. She closed her eyes, pretending it was a mystery lover in some alternate world, where their joining was right. A moan escaped her lips as she gave over to the dark desire again, which only spurred him on as he thrust fiercely, pulling her back onto him to take him deeper, making her forget this was her gentle Angel. His fingers were wicked, circling and stroking, drawing her up to dizzying heights and pushing her over the edge in a shattering crash that left her panting and shaking. He took some more, the pleasure still intense as he reached his own explosive release, his teeth sinking into the cord of her neck in a primal hold that sent her over again with a startled cry.

After, he soothed her with long strokes of his warm hand, brushing her hair back, stroking down her arm and over her hip, down her thigh. The rhythmic touch smoothed the rough edges of the sinful lust that left her shaky, pulling her back from the guilt and remorse and leaving her at peace again.

She couldn't stop wanting him. He made sure of that.

All weekend long, Angel pushed her from one extreme to

another, alternately shaking her to her core and soothing her back to a peaceful state of contentment. The guilt quickly waned, replaced by a fierce craving that Angel met with fiery intensity. And every time doubt crept in, he'd sense her guilt the moment she looked at him. And he'd grab her and kiss her, all while telling her between wild kisses that what they had was right and good. But the words didn't work for her, she couldn't be convinced. So what she taught him, without meaning to, was that she responded best if he just took over, no words necessary. If he just pressed in from behind her where she couldn't look in the face of her sin.

And then the day after their sex-drenched weekend, Brad landed in the hospital, and Angel bailed.

She leapt to her feet. She didn't know what to do with all these feelings and desires Angel had stirred up, but the one thing that had made her feel good and in control was decluttering. Never mind that it was nine o'clock at night and she had work tomorrow. She couldn't possibly sleep with the chaos in her head. She still had the kitchen, bathroom, two bedrooms, and the basement. She shuddered thinking of the basement. It was Brad's space more than any in the house, and there were just too many reminders. Of course, the bedroom had its own reminders, though they'd only had one month together before he shipped out. He only got leave once a year. The very last year of his service when he'd been so close to getting out was when he was killed. She didn't dream of him anymore. Worse, his voice and features had faded in her memory.

She headed to the master bedroom and sat down on his side of the bed. She'd long since taken to sleeping sprawled across the center of the queen-sized bed, but this was the side with his nightstand. She turned and took in the long dresser with the mirror above it across from the foot of the bed. One drawer. She'd empty one drawer of his—the sock drawer. You couldn't get any safer than a sock drawer. She crossed to the dresser, opened the top drawer on his side and peeked inside at the neat rows of socks, boxer briefs, and a couple pairs of jogging pants, rolled up to fit, that he slept in. Exactly as she'd placed them before he shipped out. He'd taken only the bare minimum with him.

She stepped back. Were these things she needed to save? No. Probably no one would want these for charity either. She fetched a large garbage bag and returned. She stood there for a moment, frozen, and then shook her head. *It's just socks and underwear. Nothing's going to bite you.* She was being silly. She had many more reminders of Brad than socks. She grabbed a couple pairs of socks and tossed them in the bag. That wasn't so tough. She kept going, enjoying the soft plunk as each pair hit the bag, liking even more the nice, neat empty space inside the drawer.

Something about decluttering was really freeing spiritually. She had no idea why, but she was so glad she'd picked up that book. She kept going—socks, check; underwear, check; pants. Wait. She should donate the pants. Maybe someone would get some use out of them. She set the first pair on top of the dresser, reached in for the second pair tucked in the back, and something scraped against her hand. She felt around. Something paper. She bent down and peered up to the top of the dresser drawer. An envelope was taped there with her name printed in Brad's tiny handwriting. Her hand flew to her mouth. Holy shit. He'd left her a letter. Chills ran through her. Oh, God. She never thought she'd hear from him again. How long had it been there? Five years? Eight years? Before he shipped out?

With shaking fingers, she carefully peeled the envelope off the drawer and sank to the floor. She leaned back against the bed, staring at her name in shock before bursting into tears. It was like Brad was watching her from heaven and knew she'd gone out with Angel. Guilt and shame swamped her. He was a hero. She was a sinner. What had she done?

She took a deep, quivering breath, opened the envelope, and pulled out a folded piece of lined paper. It was dated the day before he shipped out eight years ago.

Dear Julia,

If you're reading this, I'm long gone. (On the small chance you're reading this and I'm still active duty, put it back, and we'll talk later.) Knowing you, you've left all my stuff exactly as it was because you like things to stay the same. Unfortunately, the world doesn't work that way. Anyway, assuming I'm dead (sorry to be morbid), please know that everything I did, I did for you. I knew when you were ready to go through my mess of stuff, you'd be ready to move on. I hope it hasn't been too long. Here's what I want, the last time I'll ever ask anything from you, I want you to sell the house and start fresh. I know you, Julia, you cling to the past, look how long it took you to forgive your parents. I'll always be a part of you just like you'll always be a part of me. I love you. You were always the better half of us.

Love,
Brad

P.S. Go see my parents. Get the letter taped inside the top dresser drawer in my old room. Read it with my parents. I know that's two things I asked from you, but you can't argue with a dead guy. Ha-ha. Say hi to Angel for me. He'd better have looked out for you like he promised.

She slapped a hand over her mouth. She could hear Brad's voice, clear as day, that devil-may-care attitude, the way he expressed his emotions, only rarely, but so sincerely they wrapped around your heart. She blinked a few times as it slowly sank in that her suspicions were true. Angel had hung around her the last five years because Brad *told* him to. She was his responsibility, his duty. Angel and Brad had always been protective of her. They met her when she was a vulnerable eighteen, still reeling from the shock of being adopted. Obviously she could never truly start again with Angel. He'd always see her as that young girl he had to watch over.

She read the letter a second time. Brad was still taking charge, even from the great beyond. He'd picked this house.

Now he was giving her a clear path for her life for the first time in years. She actually liked these instructions. She'd been stuck for so long in this dark little house. Brad was okay with her letting go of it. She'd sell and buy a house that she liked. A fresh start sounded really good to her right now. Filled with an almost manic energy, Julia set to work in a frenzy of decluttering the bedroom. She didn't stop until she finally collapsed from exhaustion.

The next night she went through the same routine with the other bedroom. And every time her energy flagged, she'd reread the letter, hear Brad's voice urging her to start fresh, and dive right back in. Night after night after night. By Saturday night, the house was nearly empty, just the bare minimum furniture and her most prized possessions. Except for the basement, she wasn't ready to go there, but still... enough to give her the confidence to call a realtor and make an appointment.

That was as far as she could take the moving-forward stuff, and she thought she'd accomplished a lot. She wasn't ready to see Brad's parents. Wasn't ready to be in his old childhood room again. And she definitely wasn't ready to find another letter from him. She would. She just needed more time to work up the nerve to deal with the emotional upheaval.

6

Angel stopped by Julia's place after his tutoring session on Saturday morning to have lunch with her and to check in. She'd been too tired to talk the last couple of times he'd called, and he wanted to make sure she was okay. He really hoped she wasn't avoiding him because of their first date.

He knocked and waited. He could hear music blasting from inside, the hard-core heavy metal stuff that Brad liked, not Julia. He pounded on the door. Was she sinking back into a depression over Brad? She still kept his things around, clinging to what she had left of him.

"Julia!" he shouted through the door. "Julia!"

He pounded for a few more minutes and then finally dug out the spare key from his key chain and let himself in. She froze in the living room, where she stood holding a can of Pledge, her hair up in a tangled knot on top of her head, wearing a T-shirt and shorts, barefoot in January. So many things wrong with this picture.

"Hi!" she said cheerfully. "Sorry, I didn't hear the door."

She pulled her cell out of her shorts pocket, aimed it at a brand-new speaker sitting on an empty bookshelf, and turned the music down remotely. He stepped closer. She was drenched in sweat. A flash of memory, Julia and him in a marathon sex session, fucking, fucking, fucking. His blood heated, Julia panting under him, the slap of sweat-soaked skin, her cries of ecstasy. He had to touch her. He lifted a hand and realized dimly that she'd said something.

He pushed a sweaty lock of hair away from her face. "What?"

She looked at him with concern. "I said are you okay?"

"Are *you* okay?" He forced himself to focus on her dark blue eyes, not all the slick, smooth skin exposed to his mouth and hands. And tongue.

"I'm great!"

"Were you working out?" Something was off. This music felt like Brad was here. It was fucking with his head to be turned on while seeing Julia cheerfully listening to her dead husband's music. He took off his jacket and tossed it over the arm of the sofa.

She laughed. "I know, hard to believe, right? I was cleaning and dancing in between cleaning."

"Oh-kay. Can you turn off the music?"

She nodded and shut it off.

For the first time, he looked around. Whoa. The place looked brand new. He realized the curtains were open. Sunshine streamed in, highlighting the wooden surfaces of the bookcases, coffee table, and end tables that she'd polished to a shine. Every surface was empty of its usual pile of crap. The floors were vacuumed with neat lines from the vacuum cleaner. "What is going on?" he asked in wonder.

She beamed. "I cleaned."

He went to the kitchen and did a double take. He couldn't remember the kitchen ever looking like this since she'd moved in. The small counter space had been cleared, the refrigerator door emptied of magnets and notes, and the round kitchen table cleared of papers. It was an old kitchen, updated last in the seventies, but she'd made the small space look more open, more usable. "Wow."

She giggled, a sound he hadn't heard in way too long. A carefree laugh of a young woman. It filled him with joy.

"Open the cabinets!" she exclaimed.

He did, working his way through them. Empty. Empty. A

small assortment of plates, bowls, and cups. Half of the old coffee mugs were gone. "Impressive," he said.

"Come on, check out the bedrooms and bathroom."

He followed her, peeking in at the guest bedroom that used to be a free-for-all storage space and now held a single twin bed, nightstand, and dresser from her childhood bedroom.

She waved a hand at the room. "I thought about donating the furniture, but then I thought it would show better with furniture in it."

He was about to ask her what she meant, but then she turned and gave him a full-wattage smile, electrifying him with lust. He wanted to rip that shirt off her—

"Come on!" She gestured for him to follow.

The bathroom had a new shower curtain—bright royal blue with a silver zigzag pattern—with matching soap dispenser, toothbrush holder, and trash can. "What is all this for?" he asked.

"Last stop!" she called over her shoulder, already moving on to the master bedroom.

He stood in the doorway. This was a room he felt uncomfortable entering. It felt like Brad lived in here. That was their marriage bed. "Very nice," he said.

"Do you like the new comforter?" she asked, suddenly sounding unsure.

It was very girly—purple and light green with large oddly shaped flowers. "It's got interesting flowers."

"They're not flowers. It's paisley."

He crossed back to the safe living room and puzzled over this unusual change in Julia and the house. "What's going on?" he asked when she returned.

She bit her lip, and he stifled a groan. So sexy, so blissfully unaware of her own appeal. "Don't you like it?"

"It's great. Impressive what you did in a week. What inspired it?" Some part of him hoped it was their date. She was moving on from Brad, embracing life. Maybe embracing him.

"Oh!" She went to the bookcase and handed him a book.

Rejuvenate Your Life Through Decluttering. "It's been life-changing!"

He couldn't remember the last time Julia had gotten truly excited about anything. "Yeah? Maybe I should try it."

"Oh, you definitely should! I got it from the book club. No one else was all that excited about it, but I said it's a New Year, I could use some rejuvenating."

"What book club?"

"You remember Hailey from that holiday cooking class we took at Ludbury House?" That was the historic mansion owned by Clover Park where a lot of community events were held—weddings mostly on the inside of the house, some cooking classes more recently. Festivals for various occasions took place on the large landscaped grounds.

"Yeah, I remember her." Hailey was a wedding planner and had said she'd help Julia in the love department. He'd hoped that meant for him.

"She invited me to Singles Book Club."

"Singles Book Club," he echoed. Why had he not known about this? Julia usually told him everything. Was she going to meet some guy at a book club?

"Yeah. I think she thought it would be a total meat market, but it turns out only women showed up."

He relaxed considerably. "Maybe I should join."

She frowned. "Ah, you probably wouldn't like it."

"Why not? You read life-changing rejuvenating books there."

Her cheeks flushed bright pink. Unusual that he could make her blush with how comfortable she was telling him most everything. It immediately raised his suspicions about why she hadn't told him about the book club.

"Julia," he said in a teasing voice, "what kind of books do you read there?"

The pink crept into her neck. "Fiction and nonfiction."

He stepped closer. "What fiction?"

She mumbled something unintelligible, and the pink turned to scarlet. Interesting. He stepped directly in front of her and waited. She lifted her gaze to his, her eyes reflecting a secret. He knew when she was hiding something, and he knew he could get it out of her too. "Julia," he prompted.

She looked at a point over his shoulder and mumbled, *"Fierce Longing."*

He nearly laughed. He'd heard some of the women talking about that book in the teachers' lounge. It was very racy, apparently, and they spoke of it in hushed whispers. He was having a hard time imagining Julia reading that with a bunch of other women. He didn't put it past her to read anything, she was a voracious reader of all kinds of books, just not in a group like that. She was a very private person. "I heard them talk about that book in the teachers' lounge," he said. "Pretty racy stuff."

Her eyes widened. "Really? What'd they say?" She looked away. "Never mind."

He laughed. "Yeah, really. They loved it."

She blushed some more and fluttered away, stopping to polish up the already gleaming coffee table. Something wasn't sitting right with him. She'd gone through this place in a week, accomplishing what she'd never managed in five years. Hell, eight years, now that he thought about it.

"What's this cleaning all about?" he asked.

She kept polishing, round and round. "I'm selling the house."

Elation filled him. She was ready to leave behind the house she'd shared with Brad. This was monumental. He sat on the sofa across from her, where she was still polishing the life out of the wood. He rested his elbows on his knees and spoke in a soothing tone. "That's fantastic. A big step forward for you."

She stopped polishing and met his eyes. "It's time for a fresh start. I want a house that I pick, that I like. Something modern with open spaces."

"This is all good news. What brought it on?" Was she ready for him? For them to finally be together?

She gave him a wobbly smile. "I found a letter from Brad."

His hopes took a quick dive. "Seriously? Like you just found it? Where was it?"

She shook her head, smiling to herself. "It was in his sock drawer."

"Seriously?" He was having trouble wrapping his head around the fact that she'd just found a letter five years after his death. But then he realized, she hadn't been ready to go through Brad's things until now. "What did it say?"

"I'll get it." She left. He leaned back on the sofa, stunned and wondering what this meant. Had Brad finally come clean to her? He quickly dismissed that possibility. She would've been upset, not cheerfully cleaning out the house to sell it.

She returned and sat next to him on the sofa while he read it. He finished the part about selling the house, his mouth in a grim line. Wasn't this just like Brad to try to control her life from beyond the grave? Angel could've told her to sell the house years ago, but he respected her enough to trust that she'd make her own decisions when she was ready. It must've worked, though, because Julia seemed happy to have the direction. Maybe Angel had played this wrong all along with his hands-off approach. Maybe he should've pushed her more. He got to the p.s. and was instantly enraged. Brad was sending her on a scavenger hunt of letters, hiding one at his parents' house. Everything was a fucking game to him. Then his stomach dropped at the last part where Brad mentioned Angel had promised to look after her. He had made that promise the night before their wedding, but for his own selfish reasons. He wanted to be with her. A sense of duty, even a promise to a friend meant nothing compared to his desire for her. But Julia could very easily take Angel's place in her life the wrong way.

He set the letter on the coffee table and turned to her. "Julia—"

"Did Brad make you promise to look after me?" she asked softly.

"Yes, but…" She hissed out a breath. He met her eyes with all the love he'd always had for her from the first day they met. "I would've stuck around anyway. Did you ever wonder why Brad bought this house?"

Her brows drew together in confusion before she said

slowly, "He said it was perfect for us. Nice house in a nice town."

"He wanted you to live near me in case he didn't come back. He told me that straight out. He knew I grew up nearby and had a lot of family around."

She wrung her hands together. "He did mention you had family nearby, but I never really understood that. Are you saying Brad wanted me to—"

"He wanted to make sure you were taken care of, and he knew he could count on me to do that."

She stared at the letter. "I kinda hoped you actually wanted to be my best friend."

"I do."

"But you did it out of a sense of duty." She sounded resigned.

"I did it because I wanted you in my life."

Tears leaked out of her eyes. She was still so vulnerable with all she'd been through, the grief always so close to the surface. He pulled her close, though this was how they'd gotten themselves in deep last time, the night of Brad's funeral.

She sniffled and sat up. "I really do need a fresh start. I have a master of education. I'm thinking of applying for assistant principal positions."

"Where?"

"Everywhere. Wherever they need one. A promotion, a fresh start. It sounds like just what I need."

"What about me?"

She took a deep breath in and out, then hit him with a shattering statement. "You're free, Angel. You don't have to look after me anymore."

"I don't look after you."

"You do."

"I'm here for you because I..." He stopped himself. She wasn't ready to hear that he loved her. He was pissed at Brad more than ever for fighting dirty and stealing her right out from under him, leaving him with the messy pieces in his wake. Dammit. How could he be mad at a dead man? He died a hero for his country.

"What?" Julia asked.

"Look, I'm all for a promotion, new house, the works, just keep me in the loop, okay?"

"Of course I will. You're the first person I tell everything. You're my best friend."

"See, you know deep down that I am. And no one in their right mind would stick around as long as I have out of a sense of duty."

She gave him a small smile. "I don't know. You're awfully good."

He shoved a hand in his hair. He was so sick of being thought of as the good one. Even his family had branded him angelic, calling him a priest. Fuck it. He didn't want to be that anymore. This wasn't a damn Nicholas Sparks' novel (not that he read them). This was real life! And he was tired of waiting. The time for him and Julia was now.

He gazed at her, debating his next move. He wanted so badly to remind her of what they had, to strip her naked and bury himself deep inside her, but he didn't want to push her when she was in a vulnerable state. That would just put up all kinds of emotional walls with her. She had to feel good about them together, not remorseful. They just needed to get through the last of the Brad stuff and she'd be free.

She reached for the letter and carefully folded it.

"When are you going to his parents' house?" he asked.

"I don't know. Eventually. It's hard to bring all this stuff up again. When I read his letter, I could hear him again, like he never left." She dropped the folded letter like it burned. "He must've planned this ahead of time with the hidden letters. What do you think he wants me to find?"

It wasn't his place to say, but he suspected Brad had been trying to come clean with her when he couldn't in real life. More damn secrets.

"Who knows with Brad?" he finally said.

She let out a shuddery sigh and leaned against his shoulder. He looped an arm around her so her head rested on his chest. "What would I do without you, Angel? You make everything feel more manageable."

Wasn't he such a swell guy? The good one, the nice guy, the good listener. Fuck that shit. "How about a second date tonight?"

She startled, like she'd never considered it. "Oh. I thought that last date was just pretend."

"That wasn't pretend."

"But you were in disguise. So was I."

"That was so you and I could have a do-over."

"We don't need a do-over. You're the best part of my life, and I never want to lose that."

He hesitated before he spit out his worst fear. "As a friend or…"

"Yes." No!

"But we're good together. You know that."

"Every time we've been together has been wrong," she whispered hoarsely.

He tipped her chin up and gazed into her eyes. "Nothing we do together is wrong."

"It was, it is…" She broke down in tears, and he instantly felt remorse. His own selfish needs made him push her when he knew very well this was a delicate first step for her in moving past her grief.

He kissed her hair. "I've got you."

"Thank you," she said softly.

A short while later, she fell asleep leaning against him. She must've worn herself out physically and emotionally from emptying the house of years of collected stuff. He scooped her up, carrying her to bed and drawing the covers over her. He'd waited five years, he could wait a little longer. She was making progress. He took one last look at the woman who'd stolen his heart all those years ago, looked around the one room he really didn't belong in, and headed back to the living room.

He shoved his arms into the sleeves of his jacket, silently cursing Brad out. He could hear Brad's voice again too after reading that letter. The night before the wedding, Brad had been sober and serious at his bachelor party. After everyone else had gone home, he'd asked Angel to stick around.

"I've only got a month before I ship out," Brad said.

"I know."

Brad's voice turned gravelly, his eyes watery. "If I don't make it back, will you look out for her?"

Angel felt a perverse sense of hope. Maybe Brad wouldn't come back. Maybe he and Julia still had a chance. "You know I will."

Brad slapped him on the back, blinking back tears of gratitude. "Thanks, Angel. That means a lot. I can rest easy."

"Yup."

The next day Angel was best man at his two best friends' wedding. Probably the most painful day of his life. But Julia wanted him there, and he always wanted to be there for her.

A month later, Brad shipped out. He made it to his third year of active duty before he was killed.

Then Angel and Julia had to live with the consequences of their actions.

And Julia needed Angel more than ever.

7

Angel headed to Sunday family dinner the next day, the lone single guy in a family of happily married or engaged men. He was really starting to feel like the black sheep of the family. Now that his family had gotten bigger with wives and fiancées and a toddler nephew, they always had Sunday dinner at his oldest stepbrother Gabe's house, an old Victorian in Clover Park. It was the house Angel had grown up in since he was eight when his dad married his stepmom. He'd been damn lucky to get his stepmom, a kind woman who knew how to keep six boys in line while also showering them with love. He only had vague memories of his own mom, who'd died when he was five after a long bout with cancer. Like the way she called him her little Angel—the nickname he'd been saddled with since he was born. He never tried to change that because for his dad and his two biological brothers, Vince and Nico, the nickname reminded them of her. Though he was no angel, they acted like he was. Only Jared, the stepbrother his age that he'd shared most everything with, knew the score.

He headed to the dining room, where his family was already seated—his dad; his stepmom; Vince and his pregnant wife, Sophia; Nico and his pregnant wife, Lily; Jared and his fiancée, Emily; Gabe and his wife, Zoe; Luke and his fiancée, Kennedy. It was clear as black and white which were the Marino brothers—him, Vince, and Nico were all dark-haired, dark-eyed Italians—and which were the Reynolds brothers—Gabe, Luke, and Jared, all fair-skinned with light brown to blond hair and blue eyes. Except Jared somehow got green eyes. That was everyone. Every nauseatingly loving couple.

He waved to them all and leaned down to kiss his step-mom's cheek before taking the only empty seat next to Gabe and Zoe's toddler son, Miles, who was sitting in his high chair, industriously stabbing peas with a plastic baby fork. Now that Miles was thirteen months, the family gave him a wide berth. He tended to throw food.

"Hey, little man," he said to Miles, holding his hand up for a high five.

Miles's face scrunched up, clearly torn between setting down the fork clasped in his right hand and high-fiving his uncle. Angel picked up Miles's left hand and gave him a high five that way, earning a big baby-toothed smile.

"I! I! I!" Miles exclaimed, which was baby talk for high five.

"How old are you?" Angel asked.

Miles held up one finger on the hand still gripping his fork.

"That's right," Angel said with a smile. He turned and helped himself to some chicken marsala when something hit the side of his head. "Ow!"

Miles's fork was now on the floor, from where it bounced off Angel's head. Miles smacked his high-chair tray with both hands. "Dun!"

Miles's mom, Zoe, came around and retrieved the fork, holding it in front of Miles. "We don't throw forks. That hurts. Tell Uncle Angel sorry."

Miles smacked his tray. "Dun!"

"Yes, we know you're done." Zoe scooped him up and leaned close to Angel. "Kiss his boo-boo."

Miles gave Angel a wet baby kiss on the cheek before his mom took him away. Angel was still smiling, cutting into his chicken, when his stepmom spoke up. "So-o, don't keep us in suspense. Tell us about this girl you missed Sunday dinner for."

He glanced up to find his petite blond stepmom smiling eagerly at him. He shot Jared a dark look across the table, who merely smiled serenely. Hadn't he told Jared about that date man-to-man? Did he have to pinky swear him to every damn thing? Jared knew telling their mom something like this was open season. She was dying to get her youngest settled down. Not that Angel didn't want the same thing, but he had to do it slowly, carefully, in his own way.

"Wait a minute," his oldest brother, Vince, boomed. He was a big hulking guy, a construction worker, with an equally big heart. "Are you telling me Angel faked sick last Sunday? Our sweet priest told a lie?"

"I told ya he wasn't a saint," Jared crowed, his green eyes lit with mischief. "He faked sick to get some tail."

"Jared," his stepmom said, her voice a warning.

Jared looked contrite. "I meant for a first date of a, um, relationship." He flashed a grin, pleased with his amended answer. "So when's the second date? Hmmm?"

Emily, sitting at Jared's side, smiled and shook her head. Jared was giving him a hard time because he'd not exactly been an angel when it came to Jared and Emily getting together. Translation: Angel had had a little too much fun at Jared's expense.

"Would you like to invite her to dinner?" his stepmom asked sweetly.

Angel felt bad, leading his stepmom on with her hopes to see him settled. "I'm not sure we'll have a second date."

"What're you waiting for?" Jared asked in a fake sweet tone. "Just work it out. Talk things over."

Angel scratched his cheek with his middle finger while looking at Jared. He didn't appreciate his own words of advice for Jared and Emily being thrown back at him.

Jared snickered.

"Did you ask her on a second date?" Emily asked.

His entire family looked at him with a mixture of concern

(the women) and amusement (his brothers). His dad just kept eating quietly; as usual, he left all the dating talk to his wife. Angel shoved some chicken in his mouth and chewed. Everyone kept looking at him. Finally he finished chewing and said, "I've been busy."

"Busy," Jared scoffed.

"Too busy to hook up?" his stepbrother Luke asked incredulously. "Make time."

"Yeah," Jared said, "get your head out of your ass and get some tail." He jumped. "Ow!" He turned to Emily. "That hurt." She whispered something to him, and he got quiet.

Angel shook his head.

"What's her name?" his stepmom asked.

Angel sighed and put his fork down. After all these years, and with all of his brothers happily matched up, he knew his stepmom worried about him. "It's Julia."

There was a collective gasp, quickly followed by Jared's, "I knew it!"

Angel met his stepmom's blue eyes directly. "She thinks she's ready to start dating again, so I took her out."

"And?" his stepmom asked, reaching over and giving his hand a squeeze.

"And she thinks maybe we should stay friends." His shoulders sagged in defeat.

"Bullshit!" Vince boomed.

"Yeah!" Jared said. "You show her the fun times and wear her down."

"Angel is a lot of fun," Emily said, which earned her a dark look from Jared followed by a kiss that was entirely too carnal for the family dinner table.

And then, for the first time ever, his dad spoke up on the topic of love. "Now, Angel," he started, and the room fell into stunned silence, all eyes and ears on his dad. "I have never in my life seen the kind of dedication and selfless devotion to a woman like you have shown to Julia." He paused, his dark brown eyes filled with compassion and love, all aimed at him. Angel swallowed hard. "It's been five long years since her husband passed. If you truly love her, you need to step up now or walk away. If it's meant to be, it will be." The room erupted into agreement, suddenly silenced when his dad held up a finger. "Otherwise, I want to see you find someone who will love you the way you deserve. You understand, son? Step up or step off. It's that simple."

The words hit deep. His dad had a way of wading through the muck and making everything clear. It really was as simple as that. *Step up or step off.* Angel slowly nodded. "I've got it, Dad. Thanks."

"I know you'll do the right thing," his dad said, which got Angel choked up.

His stepmom squeezed his dad's hand before turning back to Angel. "I have a feeling we'll be setting another place for dinner soon," she caroled in an unwavering vote of confidence in him.

Angel grinned and dug into his dinner, knowing his family had his back. No matter what.

~

Julia headed to book club at Something's Brewing Café, eager to share the life-changing results from the decluttering book. She may have been the only one to read the book this time, but she was sure after hearing how much it helped her, everyone else would take an interest. She just hoped they didn't get into too much nitty-gritty about *Fierce Longing*. It was so uncomfortable to sit and listen to that. She opened the door of the café and Hailey greeted her like a long-lost friend.

"Julia! You came back!" She rushed over in her bright green sheath dress with matching pumps and gave her an air kiss on both cheeks. "I was so afraid we scared you off!"

"Not at all," Julia replied. "In fact, that book changed my life."

"Ooh," Hailey said, her pale blue eyes lighting up with anticipation. "Do tell."

Julia took off her fleece jacket and headed for the circle of chairs. Hailey followed. "The book hit me on a deep level." She dropped her purse next to the chair and met Hailey's eager eyes, searching for the words to describe just how much the book meant to her. "It was like a spiritual thing. The more I decluttered, the better I felt."

Hailey deflated. "Oh. I thought you meant the dirty book."

"Did someone say erotic?" a female voice said from behind them.

Hailey turned toward the door and put her hands on her hips. "Mad! You're deliberately teasing Julia. Not everyone is as ballsy as you."

"It was dirty, filthy fun," Mad said, clomping her way past them in her heavy black work boots and over to the coffee counter. "I already bought the second book."

Hailey turned to Julia and lowered her voice. "I'm not even sure what she's doing here. I thought she was only here the first time because she lost a bet."

"You talking about me, Red?" Mad asked.

"My hair is strawberry blonde, not red," Hailey said, tossing her hair over her shoulder. "You're red." She pointed at Mad's dyed red hair.

"Next time I see you it'll be purple," Mad said.

Hailey huffed. "Whatever. Where's your brother?"

Mad's face fell, surprising given how tough she seemed. "I just…kinda wanted to talk about the Fierce book, but if you'd rather have him…"

Hailey rushed over to make amends, so Julia thumbed through her decluttering book, picking out favorite tidbits to share. Her friend, Ally, a fifth-grade teacher at the same school where Julia worked, arrived with Carrie, a young blond nurse with glasses, talking and giggling as they walked in.

"I loved it!" Ally declared. "Damon was so hot. Did you all love it?"

Julia felt heat rise up her neck and headed to the counter to get herself some coffee.

"I loved it too!" Hailey exclaimed.

"Not bad," Mad said, and when Hailey elbowed her, she grinned. "I loved it too."

"Carrie says Damon is her new book boyfriend, but I had him first," Ally said.

"It's fiction," Mad said dryly. "We can all get off to him whenever we want."

The women laughed, except Julia, who hurried back to her seat, putting her book in her lap, mentally preparing to interrupt all the *Fierce Longing* talk with her own nonfiction report.

Lauren Bishop, a teacher from Clover Park Elementary with long brown hair, arrived next. "How hot was Damon?"

"Smoking," Mad said. The women all rushed to agree, piling on the glorious adjectives—to die for, swoony, vibrator-worthy. Julia's cheeks burned an inferno of quiet embarrassment as she squashed lustful memories of just how vibrator-worthy Damon really was.

"Are we all here?" Hailey asked as the women settled into the circle of chairs with steaming mugs of coffee, tea, and cappuccino.

"Wasn't there one more?" Julia asked. "Charlotte? The woman with the workout clothes?"

"Sorry I'm late!" Charlotte rushed in wearing a jacket over leggings. Her light brown hair with blond highlights was pulled into a cute ponytail on top of her head. "Had a personal training session right before this. I'm the trainer."

"Hi, Charlotte!" Hailey said brightly. "Did you enjoy Damon?"

"Fuck me!" Charlotte exclaimed. "He's the stuff of wet dreams. Am I right, ladies?"

A chorus of wolf-whistles and "abso-fucking-lutely" rang out.

"We really need to get some male members for our little club," Hailey said, looking around. "I know it's fun with us girls, but the whole point of a singles book club is to meet someone. Since Josh isn't coming through for me, *again*, does anyone have a brother, cousin, friend, anyone at all they could invite?"

And then, like he'd been summoned, the door opened, and in walked Angel. "Is this where we get to talk about sexy books?" he asked, looking right at Julia with a devilish grin.

She instantly heated, simultaneously embarrassed and mortified to talk about *that book* in front of *him*. This could not be happening. Why did she tell him about the book club?

"Angel!" Hailey exclaimed, leaping to her feet in her excitement over his presence. They knew each other from cooking class. "You really are an angel, here to save the day. We were just saying we needed some men in book club."

He shed his black leather jacket and strutted over to the group, taking them all in with one of his charming, dimpled smiles. "I'm happy to be the token male. Call me Angelo. Angel is an old nickname."

A soft swoony sigh echoed among the women. Julia stiffened. It was one thing to set Angel free, quite another to see six lusty, man-crazy women leering at him. She knew Angel had dated over the years, even slept with some of them, but it was always done far away from her, and he never talked about it.

"Have a seat, Angelo," Charlotte purred, indicating the seat next to her.

And damn if he didn't take it. There was a seat next to Julia too, but did he want to sit next to his best friend? No-o. He wanted to sit completely across the circle where she'd have to watch—

He winked at her.

Her breath caught. What did that mean? Was he playing some kind of game? Was he going to embarrass her by talking about *that book*? Please no. Anyone but Angel.

"Would you like some coffee?" Carrie asked from Angel's other side. "I could get you some."

"I'll get it," Lauren and Mad said at the same time.

Angel held up a hand. "Ladies, please, keep your seats. I'll get it. Anyone want something sweet from the café? On me."

The six women rushed him in a mob. Julia rolled her eyes. Seriously. Were they that desperate that the first sign of kindness from a man had them falling all over themselves? She heard Angel chuckle, a rumbled reply, and then the crowd cleared as he headed to the counter. The women returned to their seats. Hailey moved to Charlotte's other side, probably to be closer to Angel.

"Is he single?" Charlotte asked Hailey in a stage whisper that Julia clearly heard across the room.

"He must be or he wouldn't be here," Mad returned.

Hailey nodded enthusiastically.

"Who brought him?" Lauren asked, taking them all in.

"I know him from work," Ally said. "Isn't he dreamy? I asked him out once, but he said he doesn't date coworkers."

"What?" Julia burst out. Angel had never mentioned that. Nor had Ally, and she thought they were good friends. They chatted every day in the teachers' lounge over lunch, and just last week Ally announced she had a new boyfriend and they were in love. "When was this?"

"When I broke up with Dean," Ally replied. That was two months ago, after Dean, her boyfriend of four years, dumped her. Ally didn't take any kind of breather between boyfriends, just dove headlong into the next one, declaring herself in love. Julia didn't think love happened that quickly or easily, no matter how much Ally sang that silly song.

"I thought he would've told you," Ally said to Julia. She addressed the group. "Julia and Angel are best friends. They tell each other everything. Well, I guess not everything."

"He's your best friend?" Mad asked. "Why don't you hit that?"

Julia stuttered, unable to articulate any kind of explanation for her relationship with Angel.

Hailey switched seats to sit next to Julia. "I completely understand a platonic relationship. That's how Josh and I are. So how did the online dating thing go? Did you find any matches?"

She glanced over at Angel chatting with Shane, owner of the café, and thought of her surprise match. Her first do-over date with Angel. "I did, but it didn't work out. I deleted my profile. Online dating isn't for me."

"Honey, you can't give up after just one date," Hailey urged. "You'll never find love that way. And isn't that our goal?"

Maybe that was Hailey's goal, the hopeless romantic wanted more weddings to plan, but for Julia, she had her hands full just getting a fresh start on her life. "I'm fine. I can't wait to share with everyone about this book." She held up the decluttering book.

Hailey leaned back, clearly disappointed. "Wait for Angelo, and then you can share."

Angelo. Her mustachioed date. If only he could really be new for her.

Angel distributed small confections to all the ladies—mini cupcakes, banana bread, and a brownie—stopping in front of Julia and saying in a firm, staccato voice, "No sweets for you."

"Ha-ha," she said. "I'm fine."

"She's eating healthy," Angel told the group. "Lost twenty pounds last year."

Julia shot Angel a dark look that he completely ignored, returning to his seat next to Charlotte. Really. Not everyone needed to know about her weight loss.

"Wow," Charlotte said to Julia, "good for you. If you want to start working out, I'd love to get you in the gym."

"Thank you," Julia said, really miffed at Angel for bringing up her private stuff. She held up her book. "I just wanted to share with you all how much this book changed my life. *Rejuvenate Your Life Through Decluttering* sounds kind of hokey, but it really works." She warmed to her topic. "As I worked through my house, room by room, tossing things that I didn't need, keeping only my most prized possessions, and seeing empty surfaces for the first time in years, well, it was like a spiritual awakening."

"Whoa," Ally said. "Really?"

"Her house looks amazing," Angel put in. "Like a showcase—gleaming wood, lots of roomy, open spaces. The kind of house you see in a magazine and want to move in."

"Wow!" Carrie exclaimed.

"It was wow," Julia said, smiling. "Like major wow. I put the house on the market. It's finally presentable enough to do that, and I'm getting a fresh start with a new house. I've always wanted to live in a contemporary style. My husband picked out the house I'm in now, a two-bedroom ranch from the fifties."

"Your house is for sale?" Charlotte asked. "What town?"

"Not far from here. Fieldridge."

"I'd like to take a look," Charlotte said.

"I'd be happy to show you," Julia replied, thrilled to already have a prospective buyer.

Angel clapped once and rubbed his hands together. "Okay, ladies, let's get to the juicy stuff. Would a guy like *Fierce Longing*?"

"Omigod, you're going to love it!" Hailey exclaimed, which sent the women off on a flurry of praise for the hero, the heroine, and all the sexy times in between.

Julia squirmed in her seat as Angel listened in his careful way to each new vote of approval before finally declaring, "That's it! I'm reading it. No one tell me any more. I don't want any spoilers."

Hailey took control of the conversation. "Okay, ladies, *Fierce Longing* is temporarily tabled. Next time we'll talk about *Fierce Longing* and the sequel, *Fierce Craving*, since you've all gotten it already. Angelo, is that okay? Can you read both books before we meet again in two weeks?"

"Happy to," Angel replied.

Shit. Fuck. No. He'd end up reading the whole trilogy. This would be so awkward. Angel, unafraid to broach any topic, would be all over this. It didn't matter that the books were dirty, he'd want to talk about them. In his sexy voice, he'd talk about symbolism, imagery, metaphor, underlying meanings. He'd read deeply. Too deeply.

"I really prefer to stick to nonfiction," Julia announced, and then ducked as the women threw pieces of pastry at her head.

"I'm afraid you're outnumbered," Hailey said, picking a piece of brownie out of her hair.

Angel met her eyes across the room, a clear challenge in them.

"Can we at least talk about decluttering too?" Julia asked

desperately. "I'm sure if you all read the book, you'd find it helped."

"Of course," Hailey said diplomatically. "The agenda next time will be decluttering results, followed by the first two Fierce books." She turned to Julia. "I'm sorry, but we definitely need to read the third in the trilogy. After that, we'll vote on the next book. Okay?"

Julia glanced around at the other women, who appeared to be at various levels of annoyance, all leveled at her in a silent hard look. "Yes, okay," Julia mumbled.

"Tell us more about the decluttering book," Angel said, rescuing her.

"Yes," she said, opening the book to the table of contents for a reminder of the principles. "Step one, three piles, keep, donate, toss." She heard an exaggerated fake yawn but plowed on. Twenty minutes later, it appeared the women were nearly catatonic with boredom. Angel was gazing at her with no small amount of amusement though she had no idea what was so damn funny. "And that's it." She closed the book.

Hailey jumped. "Okay, everyone get your copy next door."

The women and Angel headed next door. Julia stood and put on her coat. The women seemed to suddenly perk up as their voices rose to high, flirty tones and Angel's voice dipped to husky, flirty tones. She pursed her lips, annoyed that he was here, annoyed that the women were acting like he was the last man on earth they desperately had to hook, and mortified that Angel planned to join them next time. She couldn't just not show up either because Angel would needle her relentlessly about it and, knowing him, talk about the books to show her it was nothing to be embarrassed about. His social worker training had made him able to talk about most anything without a hint of embarrassment.

Hailey appeared at her side. "Julia, honey, I really think you should go back to online dating. The fact that you're too embarrassed to read this book tells me you need to get out there again. You seem…repressed. And that's not healthy."

"I'm not repressed. I just don't think it's for me." If Hailey only knew the kinds of things Julia had done.

"O-kay," Hailey sang, patting Julia's arm. "You have my number. And remember, they don't call me the Love Junkie for nothing!" Hailey sailed next door to chat with the other women, presumably urging them to try online dating.

Julia waited for Angel. He appeared a few minutes later, decluttering book in hand. She shook her head. What on earth was he doing with that? The man lived like a Spartan in a studio apartment sparsely furnished with no clutter whatsoever.

"What?" he asked with a devilish, dimpled grin.

"What are you doing with that book?"

"What everyone else is. Getting rejuvenated. What, you don't think guys can get rejuvenated?"

"I don't think you have anything to declutter."

"I could empty some cabinets." He inclined his head. "Ready to go?"

She nodded and followed him out the door. "Are you really going to read those Fierce books? They're written for women."

He quirked a brow, his lips playing at a smile. "To quote some very knowledgeable women, abso-fucking-lutely. Maybe I'll learn a thing or two."

No, no, no. Bad idea. Very bad. She stopped walking and turned to him. "Why did you come here tonight?"

"It sounded like fun, and I was very curious to get the skinny on this book all the ladies in the teachers' lounge are whispering about."

"Who? Who's whispering about it?"

"Ally for one. Principal Johnston for another—"

She grabbed his arm. "No!" Their boss, Principal Johnston, was an extremely stern woman in her late sixties. Her business suits were buttoned to her neck, like a suit of armor, with a skinny tie. Her dyed brown hair in a tight bob was sprayed to an inch of its life so it never dared get a hair out of place.

He laughed. "Yes, even senior citizens have a sex drive."

"She's married."

"So? It's fiction."

"Yeah, but…Principal Johnston? Omigod." She started laughing, and she couldn't stop. Angel chuckled and resumed walking. She kept up. "The women really liked having you at book club," she told him.

"Women generally appreciate the token male," he said dryly.

"They were asking if you were single."

"Yeah, I heard. They're not exactly quiet even when they're whispering."

"You going to ask someone out?" she asked. At his silence, she quickly added, "I don't mind."

"Maybe I will," he said darkly. "Who should I pick? The young blonde?"

"Carrie," she supplied.

"Or the workout demon with the killer bod?"

She clenched her teeth. She'd never had a killer bod by any stretch of the imagination. She had curves, but she'd never had the kind of toned lean body topped by large breasts that men seemed to find so appealing. "Her name is Charlotte," she informed him hotly. "Geez, if you're going to ask someone out, at least learn their names."

"Good tip. I'll work on that. Maybe I'll bring name tags for everyone next time. Except for you, ol' Julia."

She huffed. Really. Name tags. It wasn't that hard to remember someone you liked.

They rounded the corner to the small parking lot where their matching cars were parked in opposite rows. Angel walked with her to her car, as he always did at night to make sure she got in safely. She unlocked it and reached for the handle to pull it open when he leaned a hand against the door, right by her head, keeping it shut. A prickling tingling sensation ran down her spine. He was close, his front to her back, which did something strange to her limbs, making them heavy and weak. She slowly turned to face him and found herself in what nearly felt like an embrace.

His voice dropped to a low register that scraped against

her insides. "What's the deal with these sexy books? You were blushing like a virgin in there."

Heat crept up her neck, blooming into her cheeks. "Nothing," she managed.

"Is it talking about them in front of the group or—" his dark brown eyes were hot on hers "—are they turning you on?"

She turned her head away, suddenly breathless. This was dangerous territory for both of them. "Please. I need to go."

He dipped his head, his mouth nearly brushing her ear as he spoke, giving her a hot shiver. "I'll find out. I can't wait to talk about them with you."

"I'm not…I won't…" His eyes locked on hers, and she lost her train of thought.

"You will," he said firmly, and she wasn't sure if it was a threat or a promise. Before she could formulate any kind of response, he stepped back, turned, and headed to his car.

She sank back against the car, the cool metal welcome to her overheated body.

Holy Angelo, she was in deep trouble.

8

Julia joined a table of her friends in the teachers' lounge for lunch on Monday, including Angel, and unwittingly joined yet another hushed discussion about *Fierce Longing*. Ally was sharing with her eager audience of Angel and some of the tenured older teachers—Dana (fourth grade), Emma (kindergarten), and Suzanne (fifth)—how the book spiced things up for her and her boyfriend of barely two weeks.

Geez, if you have to spice things up that early on, maybe the guy doesn't know what he's doing. Julia clamped her mouth shut so she wouldn't blurt out her unasked for opinion and took out her salad and sandwich.

"We're in love," Ally announced, beaming her sunny the-world-is-a-wonderful-place smile. "This just clinched the deal. Compatible in every way."

The older women tittered.

"How do you know it's really love?" Julia couldn't help but ask. "You just broke up with Dean. How do you turn around and fall in love that quickly? You haven't even been with this new guy for two whole weeks."

"Julia," Angel said quietly.

"Sorry," Julia said, flushing at Angel's gentle rebuke. "I was just surprised." She squeezed Ally's hand. "I'm happy for you. Really. What's his name again?"

"It's Mark," Ally said tightly.

"I can't wait to meet him," Julia said. "Don't listen to a bitter old lady like me."

Ally exhaled sharply, making her blond bangs flutter. "It's not your fault you're a widow."

Julia blinked, momentarily stunned because sometimes it did feel like her fault. Like payback for what she'd done. A long, uncomfortable silence followed. The word "widow" had that effect on people.

"I'm so sorry!" Ally exclaimed, slapping a hand over her mouth.

Angel smoothed things over. "So about *Fierce Longing,* what appeals to you about the hero?" He took in the group with his question.

Dana, a mild-mannered middle-aged brunette with her hair in a bun, perked up. "Yeah, Ally, what's this guy Damon like? Is he rough?"

"Is he hung?" Suzanne, a practical woman in her fifties with a specialty in the science curriculum, got right to the biology.

The women giggled. Apparently only Ally had read the book.

Julia sensed Angel's gaze and couldn't bring herself to meet his eyes. She cleared her throat and looked at Emma, the only married teacher there, presumably less interested in fictional sex.

Julia tried to turn the topic. "I read a fabulous book from the same book club—*Rejuvenate Your Life Through Decluttering.* It's really been life changing."

"Hush," Emma said. "I haven't had relations with Howard in a year. The sizzle has fizzled! I think we need this other book. Tell us more, Ally. How rough is he? Like painful   or   like   pure   delicious—"   she   shivered "—domination?"

"That last thing," Ally said with a big smile. "A total alpha male."

The women chortled. Angel grinned, winking at Julia. Heat crept up her neck. Dammit! He must've read it.

"Is it okay to talk about this in front of a guy?" Dana asked.

Angel smiled widely. "I'm in the same book club. I read it. Good stuff even for a guy to read."

"Who's the author?" Dana asked, pulling a pencil out of the bun in her hair and grabbing a napkin to write on.

"Catherine Cliff," Ally said. "Anyway, there's this one scene where Damon unexpectedly comes up behind her in the morning. She thought he was sleeping, right? And she was about to get dressed..." The women leaned in. Julia found Angel watching her, biting back a smile. She shot him a dark look for teasing her, which was a mistake because their gazes locked, bringing an unwanted rush of heat just as Ally continued. "Next thing you know he's got her plastered against the wall, pinned."

Julia broke the heated connection with Angel and crossed her legs. That just made the throbbing worse, so she uncrossed them and took a long drink of cool water.

"Pinned how?" Suzanne asked. "Are her feet touching the ground? Are they facing each other?"

"Feet on the ground," Ally said. "And they never face each other." She grinned. "It's exciting. You've got to read them."

"Can anyone join this singles book club?" Emma asked. "Even married people?"

"I'm sure Hailey wouldn't mind, right, Julia?" Ally asked. "I mean, I'm there, and I have Mark. Besides, it's not exactly a singles scene. All women and one guy."

The single teachers, Dana and Suzanne, eyed Angel speculatively. Angel took a bite of his sandwich, ignoring them. They were both at least twenty years older.

"Angel's extremely popular over there, as you can imagine," Ally said.

Angel held up a hand. "I never date coworkers." He grinned. "Not that you asked. Just putting that out there." He wagged a finger at them. "I know those racy books can get you all thinking."

The women giggled like teenaged girls.

Julia took a forkful of salad. She knew he'd say he didn't date coworkers. Though he had dated her one time. But that was different. She'd known Angel forever. Still she found herself watching him, talking easily with a tableful of women, smiling his dimpled smile, his dark brown eyes twinkling with good humor, and she saw more of what the other women saw—an appealing, sexy, great guy. Oh, shit. She couldn't let herself fall for Angel. It would just be adding another wrong to all the other wrongs she'd committed. And if it didn't work out, she'd lose him for good. Like she'd almost lost him after the last time they'd hooked up. She pushed the memory deep down and focused on her lunch.

"Ally, did you get to the third book yet?" Angel asked. *"Fierce Loving?"*

"No!" Ally exclaimed. "No spoilers! I'm trying to read along with the book club."

"All right," Angel said. "Let me know when you get to it because I have some thoughts and want to hear your take on it."

Julia's head shot up, her gaze colliding with Angel's. What kind of thoughts? She didn't dare ask. His return gaze was serious and made her stomach do a weird flip.

She returned to her lunch. When the buzzer rang for the end of the period, she happily made her escape back to the classroom.

Julia couldn't help but notice that Angel walked into book club the following week like he expected the women to fawn all over him. He made a late entrance, snagging not only the attention of the usual ladies but also the teachers who'd shown up from work. He didn't walk so much as strut with a sexy, charming smile thrown to the group. He waited until he was at the circle of chairs with everyone's focus on him before slowly removing his black leather jacket and carefully folding it in half, draping it over one forearm. His black long-sleeved collared shirt with an open button on top highlighted his dark

Italian good looks and showed off his best features—broad shoulders, muscular arms, and a narrow, trim waist. His faded jeans and black leather shoes screamed hot bachelor male, and the women responded in kind by gazing at him in open appreciation. And all Julia could think was—*want*.

Dammit. Angel was making it so hard to do the right thing.

"Sorry I'm late," he said with a hint of his dimpled smile.

"No problem!" the women chirped. The book club now had ten women, the original seven—her, Carrie, Mad (who still pretended she didn't want to be there), Lauren, Charlotte, Ally, Hailey—and the three teachers from work, Dana, Emma, and Suzanne. A chorus of "so good to see you" and the like rang out, and Angel graced them all with another sexy smile. His gaze collided with hers, a glimmer of amusement shining in those dark brown eyes. She got a very uneasy feeling from that look. He was up to something tonight.

"Angelo," Hailey purred, "you're right on time. Have a seat." She moved her white wool coat from the chair next to her that she was apparently saving for him.

Angel sauntered over and took a seat. "Thank you."

Hmph. Hailey used to save Julia that seat. Unfortunately, Julia was seated across the circle from Hailey with a clear view of what would no doubt be massive amounts of flirting. Not only that, Hailey wouldn't let them start until *he* arrived. No one had read the decluttering book, though most of them had bought it. Everyone had finished the second book in the Fierce trilogy, *Fierce Craving*, and were dying to talk about it. She couldn't believe they wanted to discuss what was basically a female fantasy in front of a man, but maybe that was their way of flirting.

Hailey smiled at the group as she took them all in. "So-o-o, what did we think about *Fierce Craving*?"

The women all spoke at once.

"One at a time," Hailey said. "Let's have a civilized discussion."

Angel raised his hand.

"Oh, that's a good idea," Hailey said, gracing him with an

adoring smile. "Raise a hand to share. Now that we have some new members, it could get really noisy in here. And I'm sure we'd all love to hear the male point of view."

Angel flashed a smile, provoking a female sigh from somewhere in his circle of admirers. "Happy to share it. I know on the surface the book seems to be a sexy romp designed to get you worked up and, boy, does it deliver, but let's go a little deeper. Did anyone—"

"I don't think it's that deep," Julia scoffed. "It's about desire."

"Julia, you read it?" Hailey exclaimed.

"A bit," Julia admitted, her cheeks burning. "I didn't want to be completely lost."

Angel slid her a look before addressing the group. "Did anyone pick up on the use of light and shadow as a metaphor? The light when Mia is going about her regular life, the shadow whenever Damon's in the scene?"

"It's always dark and shadowy when they make love," Ally said. "She never knows what he—"

"Make love," Mad said scornfully. "Please, they're fucking."

"You don't think Damon loves Mia?" Hailey asked in a hostile tone. "Because, if you don't, I think you completely missed the point."

Mad straightened out of her permanent slouch. "These books aren't about love. They're about our secret cravings."

Julia fought a full-body blush and wished she'd gotten herself a cold drink instead of hot tea.

Charlotte's hand shot up. "What about the bath scene? He's so gentle, bathing her with no thought but to soothe her."

"Because he just fucked her brains out on the dining room table," Mad barked. "She's still shaking from how powerful it was." Mad suddenly flushed bright red like she was remembering the scene. "Damn. This author's good. I can't wait to read *Fierce Loving*."

"That one must have love," Hailey declared triumphantly. "It's in the title. Right?" She turned to Angel, her pale blue eyes wide and beseeching. "They *have* to have a happy ending."

"I don't know," Angel replied seriously. "Mia and Damon have some major issues to work through."

The women launched into a long discussion about those issues—Damon's need to possess Mia despite her powerful brother's threats to hobble Damon's multibillion-dollar empire. Mia's need to keep her secrets at all costs. That got out of hand, and nobody took turns talking at all until Angel finally held up a hand, and the room quieted.

"What do we think about the symbolism of the safe word?" Angel asked, his voice deep and smooth and shockingly erotic to Julia's ears.

The women tittered.

"She never says it," Lauren said. "How can that be symbolic?"

"Why won't she say it?" Angel pressed. He leaned forward, elbows on his knees, and the women leaned in. Except Julia, who became fixated on his mouth, greedily taking in the erotic words that rolled off his tongue like warm honey. "What does pomegranate mean to her? Why did she choose it and never say it?"

"Because she's hot for him," Ally said. They all had to agree.

"Duh," Mad said.

Julia said nothing, curious to hear Angel's take on it.

Angel dipped his head, conceding the point. "In ancient Greek mythology, the pomegranate symbolizes fertility, marriage, and rebirth."

"Are you saying Mia doesn't want those things?" Ally asked, her tone clearly astonished that someone might not want to get married and have kids.

Angel paused. Julia lifted her gaze from his mouth to his eyes, and their gazes locked in an electric moment as he said, "Think about the way Mia surrenders to her secret desires." Her breath caught as a traitorous heat moved from her neck to her tingling, aching breasts. "I think the safe word is another secret desire. But she won't claim it. Why?"

Julia's mouth went dry. Everyone spoke at once, breaking the tension of the moment. She let out a breath and tore her gaze away from the heat in Angel's eyes.

"Whoa," Carrie said, during a brief lull in the conversation. "I thought it was just about sex."

"Nothing is just about sex," Angel said, looking right at Julia. That traitorous heat flooded her now, tightening low in her belly, making her ache. And the more Angel spoke about the book in graphic detail, the worse it got, because it reminded her that he was a dirty talker, comfortable saying absolutely anything. She fidgeted this way and that, but nothing could stop the throbbing. The room fell silent, and she suddenly noticed everyone staring at her.

"Don't look at me," Julia said, trying for a flippant tone. "Angel's the one who wants to talk about this like we're in English lit." What she wouldn't give to be as cool as she sounded. She was sure her cheeks and neck were a bright telltale pink.

"I like the paradox," Dana said like the teacher she was. "Let's talk more about the motifs found in the first two novels of this very talented author."

Julia felt the weight of Angel's gaze as the conversation flowed in a rapid back and forth over the imagery, symbolism, and metaphors of Damon and Mia's torrid affair. She decided then and there that she would not be returning for the next book club meeting when they discussed the conclusion of the trilogy, *Fierce Loving*. It was unnerving the way Angel kept his eyes trained on her when he spoke, like he was talking about her when he said all these erotic observations. It was awkward and uncomfortable and so-o-o freaking hot.

Afterward, as she was putting on her jacket, she overheard Hailey invite Angel to stop by Garner's across the street for drinks. She couldn't help watching the exchange because Hailey was really, really pretty with long strawberry blond hair, pale blue eyes, and a stunning figure shown off in her emerald green sheath dress and heels. Julia wore her after-work clothes—a soft white sweater with black leggings. She stifled a sigh. She had no right to petty jealousy.

But then Angel surprised her by saying, "Maybe another time. Julia and I are heading out for a drink tonight."

Hailey demurred sweetly, saying, "I'll catch you next time."

Angel crossed to Julia's side and held the door open for her. When they got outside, she turned to him, "Was that your nice way of telling Hailey no?"

"Actually, I do want to get a drink with you tonight."

"And Hailey another night?" she blurted.

He chuckled.

Her cheeks flushed. "It's Thursday night." They usually hung out on weekends.

"So?"

"We usually—"

He stopped in front of her, held her by the shoulders, and spoke directly in her ear, his voice silky. "Let's do a little role play. It helps work out all kinds of issues and it's fun. Call me Damon."

A hot shiver ran through her. He was trained for role play for his job, so she knew he'd be good at it. The only role play they'd ever done was on that "blind" date, but that had been almost goofy with Angel wearing a fake mustache. She must be crazy because she was actually considering it. Damon did something for her. Big time. On the other hand, it was Angel. Her best friend. They needed to keep that relationship strong, and role-playing erotic romance would *not* help. She'd get caught up in it, she'd make her move, fuck his brains out, and then he'd bail. Barely speaking to her, barely looking at her, never touching her. For months, if not forever. At least that was what happened the last time they fucked. And the time before that.

"Come on," he said, grabbing her hand and tugging her along. They stopped at the corner, waiting for a break in traffic.

"Ang—"

"Damon."

"I really don't think this is a good idea."

His voice dropped to a husky register. He sounded like she imagined Damon would when he said, "What're you afraid of, Mia?"

She went damp. That voice. If she closed her eyes, it was like the fantasy Damon came to life. Could she enjoy Angel if she was someone else? She'd dearly love to be someone else. The weight of her past, their twisted history, was too much to bear sometimes. "Okay, I'll play but only for one drink."

They got to the bar, where Josh, Mad's older brother, was on bartender duty. "Hey, beautiful," he said to Julia with a charming smile. Heat crept into her cheeks again, unused to flirts. He was in his thirties, she figured, and it was easy to see why women found him appealing. His dark brown hair curled a bit over the collar of his flannel shirt, and some laugh lines around his warm brown eyes softened the rakish look of his scruffy jaw.

"Hey, Josh," Angel growled before helping her off with her jacket and setting it on an empty stool. He peeled off his jacket, and she was momentarily distracted by his masculine grace, the muscular lines of his arms, his hard chest, and flat stomach. She licked her lips.

Josh spoke up. "What can I get ya?"

She tore her gaze away from Angel and stared blankly at Josh.

"I'll have a beer, and she'll have a sidecar," Angel said.

She jolted. She always had chardonnay. The sidecar was what Damon made for Mia after they hooked up. It was a sophisticated drink—cognac, triple sec, and lemon juice. Damon always tasted her after, partial to the lemon flavor that lingered on her lips. Angel's heated gaze challenged her to break character, to break the game.

She straightened. "Sounds delicious."

"I think so too," Angel said and then whispered gruffly in her ear, "Mia."

Josh tapped the bar. "Got it."

Angel turned his body slightly, leaning his forearm on the bar top and blocking her view of Josh. "Why does your brother want to keep us apart, Mia? Is it because I knew you when you were just his little sister? Because from what I've seen, you're all grown up." He gave her a slow, appraising once-over, lingering on her mouth and breasts and continuing all the way to her toes in a way that would've been insulting from any other man, but instead warmed her. The Angel she knew would never give her a once-over like that.

Angel leaned down to her ear. "You have to answer the question, Mia."

She blinked. Question?

Angel spoke near her ear, the words hot against her skin. "Why does your brother want to keep us apart?"

This seemed important. Why did her brother want to keep them apart? The secrets. But had he read that far?

She met his eyes. "How far—"

"All the way," he said with a devilish grin.

She flushed because that devilish grin was pure Angel. She wasn't sure how much longer she could do this role-play thing. She should stop this game and explain how important their friendship was to her.

"Angel, you know you're my best friend—"

His fingers covered her lips, halting the words. "Damon and Mia are not best friends." His thumb stroked across her lower lip. The bar with its light and people and noise faded away. Heat pooled through her as he pressed on her lip, opening her mouth—

"Here you go," Josh said jovially, setting their drinks on the bar.

She grabbed her drink and swallowed greedily. Angel sipped his beer, watching her with a heated gaze that her body immediately understood. Liquid heat loosened her limbs, making her long for what she couldn't have. She tore her gaze away and took another long drink of her sidecar, feeling peculiar, like she wasn't herself sitting here drinking this drink that was so different from her usual. The edges of Angel's jaw blurred a little, the dark five o'clock shadow more pronounced. She found herself reaching out to stroke that stubble, reveling in the texture, rough and warm.

"Mia," he said gruffly, grabbing her fingers, sparking a dark desire. It was like the book suddenly came to life. And she wanted to go there. To fall into that story. Mia could enjoy a man like Damon. She wouldn't have to think about anything serious, only surrender to what she secretly craved. Julia thought that sounded brilliant right about now.

She flipped her hair over one shoulder, playing the coy Mia. "Who knows why my brother wants to come between us?"

He leaned close, his eyes darkening with something raw and unfamiliar. "What aren't you telling me?"

She turned away, her stomach fluttering. "I have no secrets," she said softly.

Angel's warm hand cupped her jaw, turning her back to him. "I know you do. What's it going to take to break down those walls?"

She swallowed hard, the words hitting too close to home. "Maybe they're there for a reason."

His fingers stroked down her throat as their gazes locked. She swallowed, her heart thumping wildly. "I don't care if my empire turns to ashes," he said. "I will have you completely, every dirty little secret exposed."

Adrenaline surged through her.

He leaned down to her ear. "Do you trust me, Mia?"

She opened her mouth and nothing came out.

She grabbed her drink with a shaking hand. She had no idea Angel was such a good actor, but she'd really gotten caught up in it. Like she really was Mia, fighting a losing battle against desire and what she most had to keep hidden. As if he was a dominating billionaire businessman instead of her safe best friend.

Angel gazed at her for a moment. She held her breath, unable to look away. Then he took the drink from her hand, set it on the bar, and gripped her hair in his fist, pulling her close. She was so shocked at how well he remembered the story, the first kiss in chapter one, that she let out a tiny squeak. And then his mouth crashed over hers, hard and rough, his tongue thrusting inside. Her brain shut down as molten heat traveled to dark places that throbbed and ached. His possession was long and thorough. Her surrender glorious.

He broke the kiss, his hand loosening in her hair. "I love the taste of lemon." Oh, God, had he memorized the book? That was what Damon said after the bath when he made the sidecar for Mia and told her to drink. The following scene in the bedroom was so explosive, she'd nearly gotten off right in front of all those women at the book club. How far would Angel go?

"H-how much—" she started.

"All of it," he returned with no trace of a smile.

She licked her lips, unsure if he meant he'd memorized all of the erotic scenes or that he wanted to act them all out. She flushed as he gazed at her mouth. She felt strangely out of body, both herself and not herself, with Angel and with Damon. She slid off the barstool, her knees weak.

She gripped the bar for a moment. "I need the restroom."

She made her way unsteadily around the bar to the narrow hallway that led to the restrooms and slipped into the ladies' room. It was a small two-stall bathroom, and there was a woman at the sink, applying lipstick. She smiled politely at the woman before dashing into a stall. She felt light-headed, like Angel had drugged her. No, he wouldn't do that. She was imagining things because it was so shocking how good an actor he was. How real it all felt.

They had to stop. She said she'd play the game for just one drink. They'd had their drink, it had been fun, and now they had to go back to being Angel and Julia.

She heard the other woman leave. Julia went to the sink and washed her hands, the simple task refocusing her mind. *Relax. You just had too much to drink too fast. Back to reality you go.* She grabbed a paper towel, dried off, and blew out a breath before exiting into the dimly lit hallway.

Someone grabbed her shoulder from behind and then she was pinned, the breath leaving her body in a whoosh as her back hit the wall. It was Angel, but not Angel, the dark possessive look in his eyes, half in shadow, igniting her. Her purse dropped limply from her hand as he pinned her wrists to her sides.

"Mia," he growled as his head slowly lowered toward hers.

It suddenly felt like Angel. Damon never went slow. "We have to—" The word *stop* died on her lips as he gripped her hair suddenly, filling her with desire as Damon returned.

"You don't get to tell me no. You get a safe word. Taradiddle."

She normally would've laughed at the absurd word, but there was too much Angel/Damon too close for that.

"Say it," he said, his lips brushing her ear, giving her a hot shiver, "and this all stops."

She couldn't say that absurd word. He met her eyes with a hot look of triumph before claiming her mouth with a kiss that was every bit as rough as Damon's would have been. He pinned her wrists back against the wall and pressed his body fully against hers, sealing his mouth to hers. She surrendered with a soft moan, opening for him, silently urging him on. She needed this; she didn't care how wrong it was. She needed him to be the aggressor so she wouldn't feel the shame of bringing all this on herself. His mouth moved to her jaw, his stubble scraping against her deliciously, before he moved to her ear, where he spoke in a harsh command. "Go into a stall, take off your panties, and wait for me."

She throbbed at the words even as her brain slammed on the brakes. Whoa. Wait. This was a public bathroom. Though Damon and Mia did enjoy a public fucking…no! This wasn't fiction! What if someone found them? The word came to her. "Ta-ta—"

He nipped her neck, a stinging heat jolting her into silence. His grip on her wrists was tight, determined, as his mouth continued to nip roughly along the column of her throat before sucking on the cord of her neck. Her eyes shut on their own, her resistance crumbling. She wanted him so damn much. She let out a soft sigh of surrender, prepared to do whatever Damon wanted.

And then it all stopped.

Angel lifted his head, standing protectively close, shielding her from view. Female laughter rang out as a group of women approached and then entered the ladies' room.

She came back to herself. Holy crap. What if they'd been in there fucking in a bathroom stall when a group of women discovered them? This had gone too far.

"Taradiddle," she said clearly.

He dropped her wrists, turned, and walked back in the direction of the bar.

She sank against the wall and let out a shaky breath. A few moments later, she picked up her purse from where she'd dropped it, pulled out her cell, and called him. "Who are you?"

"Who do you want me to be?" he asked darkly.

"Angel. And no more Damon." Damon made her want to do crazy things. She was still reeling from how shockingly, deliciously good at role-playing Angel was. She'd been so caught up in it that she'd almost forgotten what was at stake. Their friendship was more important than a sexy game that would only end in disaster.

"All right, come out here." His voice took on a teasing tone. "Don't be afraid of the dark Angel."

She hung up and shook her head at this surprising new side of him, rough and carnal, yet still teasing, as their long friendship allowed. She trusted him with her life. She could never be afraid of him, and he knew that.

She returned to the bar and took the seat next to her safe best friend. She glanced at him and pasted on a smile.

He did a double take. "Hey, where you been?"

And just like that, Angel was back.

What did it say about her that she missed Damon? She was seriously screwed up.

9

The next day when Julia headed to her usual lunch table in the teachers' lounge, the women were speaking in hushed tones. Angel was smiling. Oh boy. She really hoped they weren't talking about the Fierce trilogy again. She was in no way prepared to hear Angel talking about Damon and Mia while he sent her knowing looks, reminding her in his subtle way of their role play at the bar last night. They needed to have a serious talk about boundaries and lines that would not be crossed and how sex ruined everything.

And the importance of their friendship.

And how sex ruined everything.

And, most importantly, how sex ruined everything.

The last time she slept with Angel haunted her.

"I'm an adulteress in my dead husband's bed," she'd sobbed in the aftermath of an explosive release that opened her defenses and sent her into sobbing, uncontrollable tears as the grief and guilt gripped her.

"You're not an adulteress," Angel said.

"I am."

"Not anymore." Because now she was a widow. The unspoken words made her cry harder. Angel held her until she quieted and finally slept. And when she woke, he was gone. Bailing on her. Again. Just like the first time—she'd returned to campus after visiting Brad in the hospital, and Angel had disappeared.

She scowled, took out her healthy salad, and gave her lunch a good glare. She couldn't believe Angel had forgotten the aftermath of their last explosive time together. This was a very dangerous game he was playing.

"Look!" Ally squealed, shoving her hand in Julia's face to show off a diamond ring. "I'm engaged!"

"Already?" she blurted before quickly covering with a hasty, "Congratulations."

Ally, only twenty-three and way too trusting, beamed. "I know it's only been a month, but it's true love. I really think those spicy books tipped the scales in my favor. Mark is all over me every night."

"What spicy books are these?" a teacher at a nearby table asked.

"The Fierce trilogy by Catherine Cliff," Ally announced to the entire room of a dozen teachers, all women. "You've got to read them. Erotic, but in a really sensual delicious way."

"Very dirty," Angel said, making Julia blush and everyone laugh.

Ally made the rounds of the lounge, showing off her ring and singing the praises of the books. She returned to the table in triumph. "I think pretty soon we can have a book club here too. Everyone wants to read them."

"They should," Angel said, looking right at Julia. She felt herself flush and struggled in vain to hide it. Dammit.

"Will you be my bridesmaid, Julia?" Ally asked, startling Julia from her own battle of lusty wills.

She hadn't realized they were that close. "Oh. Of course."

"Yay!" Ally squealed. "It was you, after all, that inspired me to read all those books."

Julia smoothed her hair and sputtered, "I-I can't imagine why."

"Because you were blushing so much I knew you must've read the first one and thought it was really good."

"Did you read it ahead of time?" Angel asked Julia.

Julia's cheeks and neck burned. Just once she'd like to be

cool enough not to blush when she was the center of attention. "I was just as surprised as everyone else when Hailey started off with that one."

"And Angelo, will you be a groomsman?" Ally asked. "I know we're not as close as me and Julia are, but we need one more guy to even out the wedding party." Ally cringed. "That sounds terrible, doesn't it? Never mind. Sorry."

"I'd love to," Angel replied. "An honor. Thank you."

"Oh," Ally tittered. Then she spoke in a stage whisper to the other women at the table. "Too bad he doesn't date coworkers."

"Too bad," Julia muttered under her breath.

"What?" Ally asked brightly.

Julia shook her head. "Nothing." She didn't want to be a downer on Ally's bright, happy day. She was just having trouble wrapping her mind around this rush wedding. And, truthfully, she knew it would be hard to be at a wedding. She hadn't been to one since her own. One that she'd had doubts and guilt over, but had gone through with anyway.

"You should get in touch with Hailey," Julia said. "She'd be thrilled to plan your wedding at Ludbury House."

Ally pushed her blond hair behind her ears. "I already did! I called her before I called my parents. The couple that was going to be married on Valentine's Day broke up, so it's all mine! Can you believe it? I'm going to be married in just two weeks!"

"Wow," Julia said, biting back every warning about rushing into things that immediately came to mind.

Dana, Emma, and Suzanne launched into a long discussion on the wedding gown, and Dana pulled up her wedding Pinterest board on her cell phone to show Ally all the gorgeous dresses, cakes, and flowers she'd pinned. And Dana didn't even have a boyfriend. Julia's own wedding had mostly been planned by her mom and Brad's mom since she and Brad had been studying for final exams in college. She'd been finishing up her sophomore year; Brad had been a senior ready to graduate. What would it have been like to actually enjoy planning a wedding? To fuss over the details? To go dress shopping? Even for the gown, Julia missed out. Her mom had taken her measurements and had her own wedding gown taken in to fit her. Julia hadn't wanted to turn away the sweet gesture. She and her adopted mom had finally reconciled when she'd gotten engaged. In no small part because Angel had given her some tough love after she'd told him her idea about eloping since neither she nor Brad were close to their parents.

She'd never forget how harsh Angel had been with her, in a way he'd never been before, practically yelling in her face. At least it had felt like it coming from her best friend.

He'd jabbed a finger at her, standing so close she could feel the fury radiating off him. "You know what, Julia? You're going to act like an adult? Get married, buy a house, the whole deal, then *grow up* and go thank your mom for taking you in as a daughter, instead of despising her for adopting you!"

Tears stung her eyes and she recoiled, taking a step back. Angel had always been so careful of her feelings. She tried to explain. "It's just the way she hid it from me, springing it on me at my high school graduation. You know my story."

"So she made a mistake," he snapped. "People make mistakes. Move on."

He'd left in an angry rush. It physically hurt her to have Angel mad at her. But he'd gotten through to her. She realized he was right, she needed to face life as an adult now, even if she was technically still in her teens. Nineteen was legally an adult. She'd apologized to her mom, who'd promptly apologized to her, and they'd both ended up crying and hugging. They were too different to ever be very close, but things did gradually improve from there. Enough that she could truly enjoy having her parents at her wedding. Even if she was a tangled emotional mess. She knew it was far too late to back out. Her husband-to-be was going off to a war zone. He loved her. She loved him.

Julia had stood at the altar next to Brad, but all she could see was Angel, best man at Brad's side, reminding her that love didn't work in threes.

~

Julia had a meeting with a realtor early Saturday morning, who toured the house and seemed pleased with it. The woman was no-nonsense and flat out told her she'd have to empty the basement. People needed to be able to walk through the basement and imagine their own stuff there. So Julia found herself at nine a.m., girding her loins as she paced the living room before her descent into serious Brad territory. Since she had to take a trip to his parents' house soon anyway, as he'd requested in her letter, this would be a good time to gather his boxes from childhood and give them back. She should probably donate the workout equipment too, though she'd need some help hauling it up out of the basement. She called Angel for help in hauling the boxes to her car, making sure he understood she'd be going to Brad's parents' house solo, and he promised to stop by after lunch after he finished tutoring. He had three students every Saturday morning that he helped brush up on the classwork they couldn't quite grasp because of attention difficulties.

Three hours later, Julia was knee-deep in old memories, both from Brad's boxes from childhood and from her own. She sat cross-legged on the floor in her sweater and leggings, covered in dust, her eyes gritty from all the crying she'd done. She'd found her old collection of dolls, her first day of school dresses, even her silly trading cards from a fad on ugly trolls. Brad's old school pictures had hit her hard. He looked like the kind of kid who'd be tough to handle in the classroom, mischief written all over his face. Memories of him—his joking crazy ways, his wildness—bombarded her tender heart, each one a sharp stab on an old wound. He'd been so different from her, a golden god, larger than life, opening her up to parties and people in a way she'd never experienced before. It wasn't until they'd dated for three months that he'd changed, really settling down and getting serious about life. Not just about her, but also serious about school, thinking about his future. She'd found it flattering that he wanted to take his future seriously because, as he said, he wanted to be the man she deserved, even as she longed for his old fun ways. But how could she complain? A golden god had put her—plain, mousy Julia—on a pedestal. She'd never felt special before Brad. Why couldn't that have been enough? Why did she turn to Angel?

She shoved the box of Brad's pictures and report cards (none of them good) over to the long row of Brad stuff she needed to haul upstairs and into her car. A wall of Brad. She took a deep breath and turned to another box. None of the boxes were labeled, so each one was a painful surprise. She opened it and found all of his Little League trophies. A chill ran through her, and she crossed her arms, hugging herself. She should've had kids of her own by now. If Brad hadn't died, she probably would've. They'd talked about that. She wanted kids of her own so badly. He would've gotten out of the army at twenty-five. She would've been twenty-three. Their child would've been five. Maybe in their first year of Little League.

A voice spoke through the thick silence, startling her. "We should give all these boxes back to his parents." Angel. She relaxed, knowing he'd share the burden with her. He was her rock.

"I will," she said, giving him a grateful smile for showing up. "Thanks for coming."

"Of course." He crossed to her, peeked in the box that had made her falter with could-have-beens, and closed it up. "I got it. I'll put these in your car."

She nearly wept with relief. "Thank you."

He made short work of it, carrying two or three boxes stacked at a time, ten boxes in all. So far, anyway. He returned downstairs with two glasses of water and handed her one. She drank greedily, parched from her work and from crying.

"I couldn't fit it all in your car, so I put some in mine too," he said. "I'll go with you."

She shook her head. "No, I told you I need to do this on my own. I'll rent a van." She was supposed to read Brad's letter with his parents. She didn't want Angel to have to go through that or deal with the aftermath of whatever it said.

"You sure?"

"Yeah. Remember the letter?"

"Fucking Brad," Angel muttered. He took a long drink of water.

She drank too, the cool liquid easing the tightness in her throat. "I just have to get it over with. I'm already worked up, going through all this stuff. I'm heading up there tomorrow."

"You still in touch with his parents?"

She nodded. "I talk to his mom regularly. She's still having a hard time. He was an only child. Like me."

Angel took their empty glasses and set them on the floor near the stairs, out of the way. "So where do I start?"

She waved a hand at the mess of boxes she still had to go through. They were lined up as tall as she was in three rows. "None of them are labeled. The movers packed everything for us. Just open a box and, if it looks like his stuff, put it over there to go to his parents. My stuff I'm either going to donate or put in one of these two containers." She pointed to the empty clear plastic boxes. "No more hanging onto the past than that. It's one of the principles in that decluttering book."

He opened a box. "You sure liked that book."

"I think I just needed a push to come out of my dark little cave."

"It's definitely brighter upstairs," he said, reaching into the box. "Oh, wow. Julia."

"What?"

"You kept this?" He held up a fat peppermint stick with a small folded card. He'd given it to her early December of her freshman year. She'd never forget the simple message— Merry Christmas, Love, Angel. Back then she'd spent a lot of time reading that little card, marveling at the "love" part. She and Angel had barely spoken beyond a quick hello and goodbye at the time because she'd started dating Brad, and Brad and Angel had a big fight and weren't speaking at all. Something about that little card wrapped around her heart and squeezed. She'd gone to his dorm room to thank him, and he'd blushed furiously, saying it was nothing, which made her blush furiously because she'd thought it meant something. She'd felt foolish and left. But she'd kept it because it gave her a warm glow every time she looked at it.

Angel's voice came out hoarse. "I can't believe you kept this."

She forced a laugh. "I'm a hoarder."

He stared at it. "It's pretty well preserved considering it's ten years old. Just a little bit of the red melted into pink. You remember what the card said?"

"Of course."

Angel gave her a strange look somewhere between wary and curious. He set the gift back in the box and slowly made his way around the mess of boxes and over to where she sat on the floor. He reached for her hands and pulled her up to stand. His expression was serious, his dark brown eyes searching hers. "Tell me what it says."

"Merry Christmas, Love, Angel," she answered without hesitation.

He took a staggering step back like she'd shoved him. He plowed both hands in his hair. "If it meant so much to you that you kept it all this time, then why didn't we happen back then?"

She felt herself flush. "I, well, you said it was nothing. Remember? I thanked you and—" her voice dropped to a whisper "—you said it was nothing." Her cheeks and neck burned, embarrassed all over again at the silly hopes of a freshman who'd never had a boyfriend, let alone two guys she adored.

She lifted her chin and met his eyes, so tired of the way the past tortured her in so many ways, big and small "I didn't want to be an idiot and read more into it than there was."

He closed his eyes as if the words pained him.

"Angel?"

He pinned her with a hard look. "You know what Damon would've done that day?"

She took a careful step back.

"What I *should've* done?" he asked harshly, the words scraping across her already raw nerves.

"Don't be mad at me," she said, her voice barely above a whisper as he crossed into her personal space and backed her up. She bumped against one of the metal floor-to-ceiling support poles for the house, and he drew her arms behind her back, capturing her wrists in one hand, pinning her in place.

His other hand held her chin and tilted her head up. "I'm not mad at you." His lips brushed across hers, making her knees weak. "I'm mad at myself."

This was a bad idea. She was an emotional wreck, knee-deep in murky heart-wrenching Brad territory, which was no place for Angel. And they hadn't had that talk yet. She'd meant to broach the sex-ruins-everything topic today, but the realtor sidetracked her with all of this basement crap. They couldn't talk here. They needed to go upstairs into the light.

"Angel," she said softly, "this isn't a good time or place for—"

"It never is," he said darkly before sliding his hand into her hair and cupping her head.

"Don't," she whispered. His grip on her hair tightened and an electric jolt of undeniable lust shot through her.

"Don't doesn't stop Damon. Remember taradiddle? That's what stops Damon."

She'd looked it up. Taradiddle meant fib. He was calling her a liar, and she was, her body traitorous as always to her mind, denying the truth of what she craved.

His eyes were hot on hers. "Say it," he demanded.

She kept her mouth shut, her body aching for his touch.

His mouth met hers in a rough kiss, his grip tight on her wrists. She couldn't fight this fire that raged between them, only surrender. Sweet, sweet surrender. He pressed closer, his hard planes fitting perfectly against everywhere she ached. With her eyes closed, she could forget everything—the basement and her memories, her best friend. This was just two bodies hungry for each other like Damon and Mia. He became more aggressive, his tongue delving, his hand leaving her head only to lift her leg, pressing them closer together, pelvis to pelvis. She mewled with need, desperate for more, rocking her hips mindlessly against his hardness, his heat. He lifted his head, his hand still restraining her wrists behind her back.

"Say you want me, Julia. Me, Angel."

She opened her eyes, and reality came back in a rush—the boxes of her and Brad's life surrounding them. The importance of never losing her best friend. Her dirty little secret.

She swallowed over the lump in her throat. She couldn't say the words he wanted.

He released her leg and her wrists, bringing a cool rush of space between their overheated bodies.

"Say it," he demanded, the tone just as angry as he'd been that day when he'd told her to grow up. She could count on one hand the number of times Angel had been angry with her. It cut deep, making her eyes hot and her gut churn. No one meant more to her than him, but she couldn't give him what he wanted either.

She closed her stinging eyes. "Taradiddle."

He let out a stream of curses, turned, and stormed out.

"Wait! Angel!" She rushed up the stairs and caught him by the sleeve as he was reaching for his jacket in the living room. "Don't be angry with me. Please. We should talk."

He turned, his jaw tight, the anguished look in his eyes reflecting the pain she felt every time she tried to move forward with him. "Why, Julia? Why can't I have you as myself?"

The weight of the past made her shoulders droop. "We have too much history."

"Bullshit."

The word hit her like a slap. She rocked back on her heels, needing distance yet needing to be close at the same time. That was always the push and pull she had with Angel. "We got together for all the wrong reasons." The guilt over that still stopped her in her tracks. The aftermath nearly destroyed her.

He stared at her for a long tension-filled moment before finally saying in a carefully controlled voice, "And what would be the right reasons?"

"I don't know!" she cried.

"Turn around," he said, his voice calm and sure and not nearly as furious as it had been a moment ago. Her mind was having trouble deciphering the change in tone.

"Why?"

"Just do it."

She turned. A moment later she felt him close, his heat at her back, and then he swept her hair to the side and his lips met the side of her neck in a hot, open-mouthed kiss. She stiffened, and he wrapped his arms around her, pinning her arms to her sides as his mouth became rougher on her neck, biting and sucking and soothing with his tongue. She moaned, she couldn't help it. He kissed up the column of her throat to her ear and onto the sensitive underside of her jaw, his grip on her loosening enough to enfold her in his arms.

His voice was husky in her ear. "If this is what it takes, then this is how we'll be."

"I-I don't know what you mean."

He lifted her hair and kissed the back of her neck, bringing hot shivers before shifting to the side of her neck. She closed her eyes and tilted her head, giving him open access. His mouth moved to her ear, tugging her earlobe between his teeth. "You need to be like Mia, only taking her lover from behind because she can't accept who she's with. Not with her secrets, not with the betrayal that would turn him against her forever."

The words hit too close, too sharply, twisting in her gut. "I don't want to play this game," she whispered.

He turned her head just enough to claim her mouth in an overwhelming, drugging kiss. "This isn't a game. Not anymore."

"Ang—"

His mouth covered hers again, silencing her. Then he was back to kissing her neck, the rush of rough possession allowing her needy body to silence her brain's protests. He tugged her hips back against him as he bent her over, pressing her palms against the wall in front of her. She was suddenly light-headed, dizzy with lust, and desperate for what he could give her. He nudged her legs apart with his leg, spreading her open to him, and then pressed his hardness against her through the thin fabric of her leggings, drawing a soft moan from her. Her body craved him, and she wouldn't stop him again. She waited in breathless anticipation for him to rip her clothes off.

He pulled away. "That's all you get for today."

And then he left her aching and wondering which outcome would've been worse—if he followed through or if he didn't.

Because she wasn't so sure anymore.

10

Angel didn't return to Julia's house that weekend. He'd pushed things as far as he could without crossing the line that always made Julia push him away. Like they were sinners. Maybe they were once, but not anymore. In any case, he couldn't spend another minute with her and not have her naked. He wanted her too damn much. So he had to keep his distance. For now.

His family was strangely quiet about Julia during Sunday family dinner. He'd thought for sure there'd be follow-up questions after his dad's advice to step up or step off. It was so unlike his brothers not to tease and harass, he suspected someone, probably his dad, had told everyone to shut their trap where Julia was concerned. He appreciated it, whoever was behind it. The situation was precarious and not open for public discussion. By Monday, he couldn't wait to see her again. That was how it always was with Julia. He could never stay away long. Luckily, they worked at the same school, Eastman Elementary, so he caught up to her in the hallway on the way to lunch in the teachers' lounge.

She walked head down, like she had a lot on her mind, and he remembered belatedly that she was supposed to visit Brad's parents yesterday.

"Julia, how're you doing? How'd it go at Brad's parents' house?"

She raised her head, and he read pain in those dark blue eyes. "I didn't go."

"Why not?"

"There were still more boxes of his in the basement, and I couldn't get the van until this weekend."

He rubbed the back of his neck, feeling guilty for bailing on her because of his uncontrollable lust. "I should've stayed and helped you finish up the boxes."

She shook her head. "I think you left at the right time."

"I—"

"Not here," she said and pulled open the door to the teachers' lounge. She was right. This wasn't the place for a conversation that could get heated.

He joined her at their usual table with Ally, Dana, Emma, and Suzanne. The women were all abuzz about Ally's wedding.

"Can you two make it to rehearsal the Friday before?" Ally asked, looking at him and Julia. The wedding was two weeks away on Valentine's Day.

"Of course," Julia said.

"Wouldn't miss it," Angel said. He wondered if he'd be paired with Julia. If he'd get to walk down the aisle with her like it was their wedding. He tuned out as the women discussed bridesmaid dresses and corsages, until Principal Johnston stopped by, and they all quieted.

"How is everyone today?" Principal Johnston asked, standing next to their table in her usual gray business suit. The principal, Carol, was stern and rigid, and typically didn't bother with being friendly in the teachers' lounge. But Angel saw a different side of her in their mutual dealings with families in crisis. Her compassion and devotion to the children's well-being first and foremost made him happy to work here. He'd previously worked for the county in some deeply troubling situations with very little support from above.

"Good," Angel responded to Carol with a smile. The rest of the women's responses were lukewarm at best. Except

Ally, whose enthusiasm for all things wedding could not be dimmed.

Ally beamed. "We were just discussing my upcoming wedding."

"Oh, I see. And you're all invited?" Carol straightened her already rigid spine.

"You're welcome to come too," Ally quickly said.

"Thank you. I will have to check my calendar." Carol abruptly took a seat and whispered, "Has anyone read the third book of the Fierce trilogy yet?"

The other women denied it, perhaps the truth, perhaps not wanting to discuss it with their boss.

"I did," Angel said.

Julia twirled a lock of her hair and looked everywhere but at him.

Carol spoke in a stage whisper. "Can you believe what—"

"No spoilers!" Ally said, covering her ears. "La-la-la! I was too busy planning the wedding to read it, but I have it and I'll finish before our next book club meeting."

"Oh, I see," Carol said, pursing her lips and taking them all in. "You have a book club. How nice."

"You're welcome to join us," Angel said.

The women leveled him with lethal looks. They, apparently, didn't want to discuss sexy books in front of their boss, but, come on, it was obvious Carol enjoyed the books and wanted to join them.

"If you don't mind me joining you," Carol said with an unusual softness to her voice.

An awkward silence fell.

"We'd love to have you," Angel said.

The other women continued shooting him death-ray looks until Carol looked around the table for confirmation. The women slapped smiles on their faces with a chorus of agreement.

Ally's smile was just as pasted on when she said in a forced cheerful voice, "This'll be fun."

Carol nodded once. "See you then." She left, and there

was a collective sigh of relief when the door of the teachers' lounge shut behind her.

"Nice going," the normally mild-mannered Dana spat at him.

Angel held up a hand. "It's not easy to be the boss. No one ever wants to pal around with you."

"For a reason," Emma snapped. "You think I want her knowing how much these books have spiced up my marriage?"

"Or led to my marriage?" Ally asked.

"Maybe she needs to spice up her marriage too," Angel declared. Then he looked right at Julia, in a look meant to eat her up, as he asked, "Who knows what Damon will do next?"

Julia's bright pink blush was all the encouragement he needed.

Hailey called for an early meeting of the book club (instead of their usual every two weeks meeting) both because she was frantic planning Ally's Valentine's Day wedding and because she'd received numerous calls from members who'd read the last in the trilogy, *Fierce Loving*, and were dying to talk about it. Julia found herself in an internal battle over whether or not to go. On one side, her brain screamed *do not go!* Listening to a discussion of *Fierce Loving* that included Angel and her boss would be excruciating (for two very different reasons). On the other side, she was really curious to hear what people thought of it.

Okay, she wanted to hear Angel's take on it. No matter how difficult that was to hear.

When Julia arrived, everyone was already there, the usual members, Angel, her teacher friends and her boss. Why Angel had to invite Principal Johnston was beyond her. The woman looked every bit as intimidating as she did at work, still wearing her uniform of a gray blazer and skirt. The only one missing was Ally. Everyone held a bright red paperback.

Julia took a seat next to the nice nurse Carrie. Unfortunately she was forced to sit once again across from Angel, who was seated between Charlotte, the personal trainer with the perfect body, and Principal Johnston. Charlotte had passed on buying Julia's house because she'd found a place she liked closer to work. Julia stifled a sigh. She really didn't like sitting across from Angel because it gave him way too many opportunities to pin her with his dark bedroom eyes as he made his erotic observations. She couldn't help the pink that inevitably flooded her cheeks, giving away the power of those words. It was extremely embarrassing in front of the other women.

She didn't miss that Angel had dressed to impress. Instead of his usual button-down shirt and khakis for work, he'd changed into a snug white long-sleeve shirt with jeans and a black leather belt, looking like a model for all-American sexy male. Clearly he was enjoying all the female attention, as he was all smiles for Charlotte and hadn't bothered to say hi to his best friend.

"What book is that?" Julia asked Mad, who was scowling as she stared at it.

Mad harrumphed. "Hailey's making us read this crap." She held up the book with gold lettering on the title, *Getting from Meh to Yeah: Your Guide to Dating in the Modern World.* Julia got a sinking feeling. This was going to be even worse than the Fierce trilogy. Hailey would probably want to talk about all their *meh* experiences and how to improve them. Julia didn't have any *meh* experiences. She'd only been with two men, both of whom treated her like a jewel. Maybe that was all she would ever get because if most people had *meh,* enough to write a book about it, she'd already had more than her fair share of *yeah* experiences.

"Just the single ladies," Hailey caroled. "And you, Angelo, since you're single."

Angel inclined his head and started thumbing through his copy.

Hailey handed Julia her copy. Principal Johnston laughed, a rusty sound like she didn't do it often as she peered over Angel's shoulder, reading along with him. Julia shot Angel a dark look for inviting their boss. He met her eyes and one corner of his mouth lifted. He thought it was super funny that their boss was reading erotic romance right along with them. Wrong on *so* many levels.

Principal Johnston waved a hand toward the dating book. "Ed and I used to be romantic like this when we first dated. He always brought me a flower. Turned out he picked it from his mother's flower bed, and she'd given him hell for destroying her prize roses."

"Aww," the women chorused.

"That's really nice, Carol," Angel said. He was comfortable talking to anyone, even a boss, on a personal level.

Carol let out a wistful sigh. "I haven't gotten a flower from him in twenty years."

"Maybe you could ask him for one," Angel suggested.

The women all rushed to disagree. Even Julia, with her limited experience, knew that was wrong.

"If you have to ask, it doesn't count," Julia said.

"Really?" he asked, seeming surprised to hear this.

"Really," everyone chorused back.

Angel leaned back in his seat, crossing his legs at the ankle. "You know what? I can't wait to dig into this dating book. I need to hear the women's point of view on what they really want." He pinned Julia with another scorching hot look. She lifted her hair off the back of her neck to cool off. They really needed to have that talk about boundaries. He'd made himself scarce this past weekend, and she hadn't pushed the issue because she thought maybe they needed some space. Then she'd been too busy after work. Tonight, after book club, they'd talk. But what if she was revved up thinking of Damon?

Tomorrow night. Yes, Friday would be good. Saturday she had to go to Brad's parents' house and knew she'd be too emotional to deal with both a heated talk with Angel and the inevitable aftermath from her visit.

"Ooh, a guy who actually cares enough to ask what women want!" Charlotte exclaimed to Angel. And then right in front of everyone, she squeezed his bicep and muttered,

"Nice." Figured a personal trainer would be concerned about muscle definition.

Angel smiled at Charlotte, and Julia turned away. Maybe they wouldn't need to have that damn talk. Maybe Angel would just hook up with Miss Perfect Body. Which was fine. Just perfect. Nice and…no! Angel had kissed *her* and pinned *her*, and they would have that talk whether or not he wanted to follow up with his own personal trainer. Because they were best friends, and best friends talked about important issues like boundaries and not crossing them no matter how tempted they were.

Ally arrived, sailing in on her happy cloud, and announced, "I loved it! This last part of the trilogy was perfect. And, omigod, that dresser scene!"

Julia squirmed, unable to help herself, and felt her cheeks burning again. Leave it to Ally to jump right in with the erotic book. The women all began speaking at once.

"One at a time," Hailey barked. "Me first." She looked around the room, taking them all in with a small smile. "What a nice crowd. Please bring your single male friends, brothers, cousins, whoever next time. Okay, back to *Fierce Loving*, do you all remember what Angelo pointed out, about the light and shadow, about how Damon always takes Mia from behind?"

"Oh, yeah," Angel said in a suggestive voice, making the other women laugh. Julia's pulse raced.

Hailey went on. "And then, after she confides her secrets, how she'd once spied on Damon's company and told her brother insider information, how Mia turned to face him when they made love?"

Mad piped up enthusiastically. "And you realize that it wasn't Damon who made her always give him her back. It was Mia who demanded it from the very first time he tried to kiss her, years before the story began, while she was spying on his company as an intern."

Angel raised a hand, and the women turned to him as one. "When Mia finally faced Damon, opening herself fully to being with the man she'd always wanted, what happened?"

His gaze locked on Julia's, and her mouth went dry. She licked her lips, watched Angel's eyes darken in response, and shivered.

"There was light!" Carrie exclaimed.

"There was light," Angel confirmed with a quick glance at Carrie before resuming his gaze on Julia. "The sun came out, and she opened all the curtains. They made love facing each other in the healing afternoon light."

There was a collective sigh. Julia couldn't speak, but the warmth of Angel's words melted her insides, enthralling her. Healing afternoon light. She loved that turn of phrase, could picture it perfectly like a golden aura around Mia and Damon.

"It was beautiful," Mad said, rubbing her wet eyes with a fist. At the collection of shocked expressions, she tossed her recently dyed purple hair. "What? I have feelings too."

"I don't know," Principal Johnston said matter-of-factly, "I missed the illicit dark scenes."

"But that's all they were," Hailey said, gesturing wildly. "Like the first two books, *Fierce Longing* and *Fierce Craving*, were all dark, all sex. They needed the light for loving." She turned to Angel. "Gosh, Angelo, I don't know if we would've picked up on that light metaphor if you hadn't come along. Thank you."

Angel flashed a devilish dimpled smile. "I'm sure you smart ladies would've figured it out." He paused and pinned Julia with a knowing look. "Especially Julia. She minored in English lit."

Julia waved that away, mortified to be the center of attention. "I was so busy with my decluttering book, I didn't give any thought to the Fierce trilogy at all." But she secretly loved it. She just didn't want to talk about it while she was throbbing in front of a group of women and especially not in front of Angel, who could read her too easily and would call her on it.

The women launched into a discussion of Damon, debating what was so appealing about him and if he was better than other book boyfriends, while Julia listened without comment.

Finally Angel interrupted with a question. "As a guy who's not an alpha or a billionaire, I'd really like to know, what's so appealing about that?"

Charlotte put a hand on Angel's upper thigh and purred, "I suspect you have some alpha in you."

Julia knew he did. He'd been so alpha as Damon, so wicked. She tore her gaze away from Charlotte's hand on Angel's leg, which he was not pushing away, and a buzz of adrenaline surged through her, urging her to bolt. She didn't want to hear Angel discussing the deep, dark desires of women, and she really didn't want to watch Angel with Charlotte.

"It's just a fantasy," Principal Johnston said.

Julia hesitated, not wanting her boss to see her fleeing the scene and wonder what the hell was wrong with her.

"I think it's our brain wiring," Suzanne, ever the science teacher, said. "Simple biology. We needed men to be the warriors and go hunt. Some part of us responds to that caveman appeal in the bedroom."

"Good to know," Angel replied, his slow sexy smile leveled right at Julia. She shot out of her seat, drawing everyone's attention.

She grabbed her jacket and purse, turned, and spoke in a rush of explanation. "I need to straighten up at home for an open house on Saturday and prepare tomorrow's lesson. Lots to do. Good seeing you all."

She rushed out the door like Damon himself was on her heels.

11

Julia headed to Brad's parents' house two days later, Saturday, with a rental van full of his boxes. She thought she'd be worked up, crazy with anxiety for what waited for her there, but instead she was numb. She could only sustain a high level of anxiety for a week, it seemed, before she wore herself out. The realtor would be showing her house to prospective buyers all day while she was away. Unfortunately, Angel had some kind of family thing last night that he couldn't get out of, which meant they'd have to have that boundaries talk tomorrow. She anticipated today would be horrible but necessary. Sort of like all of her moving-forward stuff.

She'd get through it. Hell, she'd come this far, right? She'd gone through Brad's stuff, put the house on the market, and she was putting out some feelers for assistant principal positions. Not her dream job, but it would change things up. Sometimes you just needed to kick-start your life. She smiled ruefully to herself. Sure, it had taken her five years to do anything at all, but now she was on her way.

The hour drive was easy, mostly highway, and the enormity of it didn't really hit her until she pulled into the driveway of the well-maintained colonial. Suddenly she was racked with nerves and wishing she'd taken Angel up on his offer to go with her. She forced herself to take a deep breath, anxiety always made her hold her breath, and got out of the car.

Brad's mother, Donna, greeted her at the door with a watery smile and then pulled her in for a tight hug like Julia was a long-lost daughter. She hadn't visited in more than a year, though they did speak on the phone regularly. Donna had aged significantly after Brad's death, her blond hair turned white, her back was stooped, and deep lines had formed around her mouth and her blue eyes. Julia might not have changed tremendously on the outside, but she felt a similar aging had happened on the inside.

"How are you, honey?" Donna asked, holding Julia by the upper arms and studying her face.

"I'm good, Donna. How are you?" Julia never could bring herself to call her Mom. Even Donna was difficult for her to say since she'd first met her when she was so young. But the familiarity made Donna happy, so Julia forced herself to say it.

Donna dropped her hands and stepped back. "I'm hanging in there. So you're really selling the house?"

Julia nodded. "I'll pay you back your share, of course." Brad's parents had given him the down payment.

"Not at all. That was our wedding gift to you. We're just glad you're here."

"I wanted you to have his things. He had a lot."

Mr. Turner, Ken, she reminded herself, stepped into the foyer. She took in his cardigan sweater and neatly pressed pants as he put a comforting arm around Donna in her conservative floral blouse and tailored pants. Brad was so different from his parents, both serious-minded psychologists. He'd been a bundle of uncontrolled energy, firing all over the place as he bounced from one thing to another until he joined Army ROTC and became very serious. The change in him had been startling.

Ken gave her a peck on the cheek. "Julia, how are you?"

"Good, thank you."

He pressed his lips tightly together. "I'll get the boxes."

"We'll all help," Donna said. "No one has to do this alone."

The three of them made short work of it. Fifteen boxes in all, stacked in a spare room upstairs. "That boy kept so much junk," Ken said, pulling a white handkerchief from his pocket and wiping his eyes.

Julia took a deep breath. She knew they'd want to look through the boxes, but there was one more thing she had to do. She hadn't told them about the letter over the phone. They were supposed to read it together, according to Brad's instructions, but she wanted to read it first to deal with her own reaction privately. She'd call them in to read it with her once she was sure she could hold it together enough to share that heart-wrenching rush of remembrance.

"Can I have a moment alone in Brad's room?" she asked.

Donna squeezed Julia's shoulder gently. "Of course. Take as long as you need. I'll make some tea and wait for you downstairs."

Ken stood frozen in the spare room, staring at the boxes, not seeming to notice when she and Donna left the room.

She pushed open the door to Brad's room. It looked exactly like it had when she'd first seen it. The room of a teenage boy—blue walls, blue plaid comforter on the bed, posters of NBA players, along with a pullout poster from the swimsuit edition of *Sports Illustrated*. His shelves held auto-graphed baseballs, some books about sports, and a collection of comic books. She stared at the tall chest of drawers and slowly crossed the room to stand in front of it. Her hands were shaking. She closed her eyes and tried to summon a mental picture of a smiling Brad, the way he'd been before the military, but what came to her was Angel staring at her with those deep brown eyes, silently standing by, supporting her. She opened her eyes as a calm came over her and eased open the top drawer. It was empty. Not too surprising. He'd taken most everything with him when they got married. She bent and peered up at the top of it. Another envelope with her name printed neatly on the front. Her heart raced despite expecting it. Something about seeing her name in his writing after all these years was jarring. She took another deep breath before carefully peeling the envelope off.

She crossed to Brad's twin-size bed and sat, staring at the neat handwriting with her name. She shivered, sensing his presence here. She pulled out the letter on the same lined paper as the other letter, and began to read. Brad's voice in her head was so clear it was like he was sitting right next to her on the bed, grinning his mischievous smile, talking to her.

Dear Julia, Mom, and Dad,

If you're reading this, it's probably been a while, and you've made me out to be some kind of saint. I was always a screwup. I know it. I didn't care about anyone but myself. Mom and Dad, I'm sorry for all the trouble I caused—the wrecked car, the accidental fire in the garage (at least I didn't get a drug charge on that one), trashing the house when you were away, my bad grades, back talk, and general lack of respect. You should've shipped me off to military school. Ha-ha. I put myself there, huh? My life changed when I met Julia, and I tried to be the man you raised me to be. Thank you for your valiant efforts on my behalf. Please remember me best for my charming recklessness, which is probably how we all found each other in this predicament. Donate my stuff and turn my old room into a home gym or a secret sex club. I don't care. Just don't make it a freaking museum. Love you both. Now say goodbye to Julia. She needs the push to move on.

Julia, this is called closure according to my psychologist parents. Get my baseball card collection back from Angel, empty the box, and read the letter I taped to the bottom <u>with</u> Angel. And don't make that face. You have to follow a dead man's last request(s).

Love,
Brad

. . .

P.S. Julia, I'm sorry I never told you this, but here goes—I lied about being adopted. I wanted you to go out with me, so I made that up, and it meant so much to you that I never told you the truth. These are my biological parents.

Julia's hand crumpled the note involuntarily, the room swam in front of her eyes, and then everything faded to black.

The next thing she knew, someone was pressing a cool washcloth to her forehead and brushing her hair back from her face. "Julia, come back to us," Mrs. Turner said. "Come on, honey, open your eyes."

Julia licked her dry lips and slowly opened her eyes. "What happened?"

Mr. Turner stood nearby, looking concerned.

"You passed out," Mrs. Turner said. "Have you been sick?"

She jackknifed upright as it came back to her, her head spun from the movement, and a ringing in her ears drowned everything else out. She could see Mrs. Turner's lips moving but heard nothing. *He lied! He lied! He lied!*

And then she was being lowered back to the bed, and the room came back into focus. Brad lied about being adopted. Thank God she'd never mentioned it to his parents. That shared feeling of abandonment, of never fitting in with their families, was what had bonded her and Brad together. It was why she'd chosen him when she'd been drawn to both men, him and Angel.

She'd based her entire life around a lie.

The letter. Where was the letter? She eased herself up and found it under her hip. "He left a letter. For all of us. I read it first. I'm sorry. I needed a moment with him."

"A letter?" Mrs. Turner asked in a whispery soft voice. She turned to her husband, tears in her eyes. "He left us a letter."

Mrs. Turner took the letter with shaking fingers. Mr. Turner sat next to her and put his arm around her as they read it quietly together.

Julia eased herself off the bed. The shock was giving way

to a whole flood of emotions, but the biggest one was fury. How could Brad listen to her all those years, bitterly lamenting her fate, while pretending to be in the same boat when he was the farthest thing from it? That sob story he'd told her about the orphanage, the foster homes, never being accepted by his adoptive parents—all of it one big lie. He'd sucked her in, and she'd fallen for it.

She stood by the doorway and looked in on the two people who didn't deserve the way they'd been treated, but loved their son unconditionally anyway. Brad had been damn lucky, and he'd thumbed his nose at all of them. "Goodbye, Mr. and Mrs. Turner."

"Julia," Mrs. Turner croaked out, "I'm so sorry. This must be such a shock to you. It is to us. We had no idea he told you he was adopted. He was such an odd child."

"A screwup," Mr. Turner said.

"We tried our best with him," Mrs. Turner said helplessly. "Please know, you don't have to say goodbye to us forever no matter what Brad said. We're happy to have you in our lives."

Mr. Turner turned to her, his eyes bleak. "You're all we have left of him."

"I'm sorry," Julia choked out. It really was time to say goodbye. She rushed back and hugged them both. "Thank you for being so kind to me over the years." She straightened and wiped her eyes. "I think, though, that closure is important. On that one point, he was right. So…goodbye. I love you."

"We love you too," Mrs. Turner said before breaking down in tears. Mr. Turner pulled her close.

Julia raced out the door, down the stairs, and made it all the way to the driver's seat of the van before she broke down in tears. She sat there for a moment, her emotions swirling through her, making her thinking fuzzy. She'd severed the last tie she had to Brad. Some part of her was proud of that. The rest of her was still reeling from betrayal.

Somehow she managed to start the van and get herself back on the road home. It was just long enough a drive to get her thinking about Brad. The first time they'd met, he'd called them both strays, said they had to stick together, two adopted kids left by their mothers. She'd thought he really understood, on a deep level, the abandonment she'd always felt. He'd played on her sympathy and used her very personal pain to get close to her. Her gut clenched, and her eyes got hot. She had to pull over before she lost it again. She found a rest stop a few miles ahead, pulled into the parking lot, and called the one person she knew would understand the pain of this betrayal.

"Angel," she managed, "it's me. I saw Brad's parents."

"I'll come over."

Her world righted itself again, stabilizing with the strong center Angel had always provided. Her rock. She quickly decided not to bring up all the stuff that would get her upset again. It was too much over the phone, and she needed to see Angel's familiar face, hear his reassuring voice, feel his arms around her to get her through it.

"I just wanted to hear your voice," she said softly. "I'm at a rest stop. We'll talk more when I get home."

"How far away are you?"

She took a shuddering breath. "I think about half an hour."

"I'll be at your place."

Then she remembered the realtor and potential buyers touring her house today. But she didn't want to go to Angel's place because that was where Brad's baseball card collection was with another letter, and who knew what bombshell awaited her in that one? He wanted her to read it with Angel. Oh, shit. Did Brad suspect she'd been with Angel? Her chest tightened, and she sucked in another shuddering breath.

"Julia? You're scaring me. I'm not sure you should drive."

"No, I'm okay. Can you clear out the people from the open house at my place? Tell them it's a family emergency and to please come back tomorrow afternoon."

"Done."

"Thanks," she choked out, "for always being there for me."

"Nothing could drive me away," he said fiercely. "Not you, not him. Nothing."

She closed her eyes and dropped her head back on the seat. "Angel," she said more to herself than to him, savoring the name that meant so much to her, "I'd better go." But she didn't. She just sat there, overwhelmed by it all.

There was a pause. "Are you sure you don't want me to come get you?"

She straightened, the small connection enough to keep her going. "I got this. See you in half an hour. Bye." She hung up and headed home.

Angel's car was in her driveway when she arrived. He must've let himself in. She hoped the realtor had gotten some leads, even though the open house was cut short. More than ever, she couldn't wait to sell this house and move on. She'd just pulled out her key when the front door opened. She took one look at Angel's sympathetic expression, and her lower lip quivered. She bit her lip, tired of crying over Brad.

He pulled her inside and into his arms. She dropped her keys and purse and wrapped her arms around his waist, burying her head against his warm chest.

"He lied," she said against his chest.

He pulled back just enough to meet her eyes. "What?"

"Brad lied about being adopted."

Angel didn't look surprised at all; in fact, he looked resigned. "So that's what the letter was. He finally told you."

She jerked away. "You knew?" The fury she'd felt toward Brad spiked as she realized the betrayal was now doubled. "How could you not tell me? What kind of shitty game were you guys playing with me? I was a wreck over the adoption thing. You both knew it! He lied and you let him! You just let me believe all this time when you knew! How could you!"

Angel pulled her back into a hug, and she fought his embrace, but he wasn't letting go, just hugged her tighter until she went limp.

"Julia," he said gently, his grip on her loosening, "it wasn't my place to say."

That just renewed her fury. "I can't believe you were in on this! Let me go!" She pulled away, and he let her.

"Don't be mad at me. Brad's the one who lied. I told him to tell you."

The rage built in her with every word out of his mouth. And she knew it wasn't all Angel to blame, but she couldn't rail against a dead man. All her guilt all these years over cheating on Brad paled in comparison to this basic lie at the heart of one of the most painful facts of her life.

"Julia," Angel said gently, "talk to me."

"I don't want to talk!" she yelled. Then she marched over to the living room, grabbed her wedding picture and hurled it at the wall. *Smash!* Then she grabbed the picture of Brad in his fatigues and hurled that too. *Smash!* She grabbed the frame of her, Brad, and Angel, the triangle that destroyed her, and went to throw it when it was snatched out of her hand.

"Calm down," Angel said, setting the frame back on the shelf. "There are better ways to handle your anger."

His stupid social worker talk infuriated her. She glared at him, marched over to the bookcase, and emptied a shelf of books with one sweep of her hand. Angel said nothing. She kept going, emptying every stupidly decorated shelf, faster and faster, flinging all the books and vases and seashells until there was nothing left. She turned to find more things to fling. There was no clutter left, but she had a lamp. She grabbed it off the end table, and Angel's hand closed over hers.

"Stop it," he snapped. "You can't sell the place if you destroy it."

"I want to burn it to the ground," she snarled, barely recognizing her own voice.

Angel peeled her fingers off the lamp and closed his hand over hers, tugging her along with him. "We're going to the basement."

She dug her heels in. "I don't want to be with Damon." That was what happened last time they were in the basement together. She was too furious to take any pleasure in anything right now.

He chuckled and pulled her with him, dragging her toward the basement. "You're not going to be with Damon."

"I'm so fucking mad!"

"I know." He opened the basement door and guided her down the stairs with him.

"I don't want to declutter," she said petulantly. She was past caring how she sounded. Her world had been based on a lie. Nothing was what it seemed.

Angel pulled her to the home gym, leftover from Brad, in the corner. The equipment had been too heavy for her to move. He held up her clenched fists by the wrists. "You are going to beat the shit out of that punching bag. We both are, and that bag's name is Brad."

She blinked. He nodded once and turned her to the bag. It was a long cylinder bag on a base, almost the size of a human body.

She gave a half-hearted punch, her knuckles stinging. Angel corrected her fingers, moving her thumb around her knuckles and shaping her fist more like a brick. "Do it like you mean it," he said in a low voice. "This is Brad and that bastard lied to you. He could've told you at any time—"

Bam! Something in her snapped and that solid punch to the bag felt so good she kept going, railing against Brad in the only way she could. "You lied to me!" *Bam! Bam!* "You jerk!" *Bam! Bam! Bam! Bam!* "I fucking hate you!" *Bam! Bam!* "I hate you, I hate you, I hate you." The punches and hate went on and on until she ran out of steam, sweaty and spent. She pushed her hair out of her face, punched one more time for good measure, and stepped back, gesturing for Angel to take a turn.

He let loose, but without all the screaming, his punches much more efficient than her crazy ones. He looked like a boxer. Finally, he stepped back and dropped his hands.

"You looked like a pro," she said.

He gave her a small smile. "I've had more practice."

She stared at her red knuckles, still stinging from the workout she'd given them. She rolled her neck back and forth, the tension leaving her body, making her drowsy.

"Come on," Angel said, guiding her back upstairs. She followed him, her limbs heavy, as he led the way to her bedroom and pulled back the covers. She got in, despite the fact the sun was still shining and it was afternoon. He followed, pulling the covers over them both, and settled behind her, one arm wrapped protectively around her. She was too exhausted to protest, even though it was her marriage bed and the last time Angel had been in here was the biggest mistake of her life.

Or maybe it wasn't.

Maybe marrying Brad was the biggest mistake of her life.

She closed her eyes, exhausted. Several minutes passed, and she slowly became aware of Angel's solid chest warming her back, his scent like the ocean, leather, and man. His hand splayed low across her belly, causing a tingling heat through her thin sweater, making her entire body ache with desire as she remembered all the times he'd held her like this, kissed her like this, taken her like this. Behind her, in the shadows.

Her shadow Angel was inspiration for every dirty word she'd ever written, every fierce longing, every fierce craving.

With Damon.

12

Julia woke with the first rays of sun through the blinds. It was super early for her, but she'd gone to bed early too. Angel pressed close behind her, his arm heavy across her stomach, his breathing deep and even in sleep. Her mind drifted, remembering this feeling of Angel behind her, fierce and demanding, shaking her perfect world and leaving her to pick up the shattered pieces. She felt the rough hair of his leg against her own bare leg and realized he'd undressed her. She glanced down at her favorite old purple V-neck T-shirt and plain white panties. Obviously she hadn't planned for seduction. But when had she ever with Angel? From the heat coming off him, he'd probably stripped down to his boxer briefs. She closed her eyes, fighting her own lustful instincts. How had she gotten here again when she'd tried so hard to give Angel his freedom? And then she remembered the letter, the lie at the foundation of her relationship with Brad, and she wanted nothing more than to gaze at the face of the man who had never, ever lied to her.

She turned in his arms and found his dark brown eyes looking back at her. Their gazes locked for a long sizzling moment. How long had he been awake, just holding her?

"Angel?"

He stroked her hair back from her face. "Yeah."

"You're Damon."

"I know…Catherine Cliff."

Her jaw dropped. He knew she wrote the Fierce trilogy? And he hadn't said a word. Her mind raced back to book club, to the teachers' lounge, to Angel talking about the books' deeper meaning all while gazing at her. She shut her mouth with a snap. Omigod, the way he'd acted out the role. He'd been *toying* with her! All the while knowing it was her. And him! She'd deliberately chosen a pen name nothing like Julia MacKendrick Turner.

"You knew?" Her voice was embarrassingly high. Nobody knew, nobody had made the connection back to her.

He stroked one finger down the side of her neck, leaving a tingling trail. "You think I don't recognize myself? Recognize us from that weekend in college? How I took you from behind? How rough and explosive and fucking hot it was." One corner of his mouth lifted. "Some of my dirty talk made it in there too." His voice dropped to a husky register, his dark brown eyes locked on hers. "Spread those legs, darling," he drawled. "That's right. A little more. Mmm…you're so wet for me. You taste so good. Easy…easy…good girl." He flicked his tongue once, triggering a vivid memory of his amazingly talented tongue that made her shiver. "Now," he growled, and her insides clenched. "Come in my mouth."

She might have squeaked.

He gave her a look somewhere between pity and amusement. "And your favorite book is *Wuthering Heights*. Catherine and Heathcliff. Catherine Cliff."

"You've known me too long." She tore her gaze away, focusing instead on his bare shoulder that she suddenly wanted to sink her teeth into, both because it looked tasty and because she wanted to divert his attention.

He tipped her chin up. "Let's finish this conversation first."

She started, how did he know? Her cheeks and neck burned, though how she could blush at this point, lying half naked with Angel discussing the erotic romance trilogy she'd written last year when all her deep, subconscious desire needed an outlet was beyond her. Angel had been involved with another woman for four long months last year. Part of her had cheered for his happiness, part of her had sunk into selfish despair. Writing had eased her guilt and her lust.

She ducked her head. "I'm so embarrassed. You were teasing me all that time with the metaphor stuff and the role play."

"I was giving you every opportunity to come clean. Why did you write it?"

She swallowed, met his steady gaze and, seeing no judgment there, blurted it all out in a rush. "When you were with your girlfriend last year and things went on for months, the craving got worse. Like if I couldn't have you, I wanted you even more." She looked away, ashamed of herself. He remained quiet and utterly still. She met his eyes again and went on. "I'm sorry. I know that was selfish and unfair. The vibrator wasn't doing it for me, and one night I found myself writing about that weekend in college, and then it sort of took on a life of its own and became something else. Its own story."

Angel didn't even blink at the mention of her vibrator even though she'd never told him about Bob the I, II, or III before. Bob the I when Brad first shipped out (and she'd almost hooked up with Angel). Bob the II when Angel had that four-month-long girlfriend. That one should've lasted longer. It must've been defective. Bob the III was still going strong.

His warm hand stroked her hair, down her arm, and finally gave her hand a gentle squeeze, both arousing and soothing her. He gazed at her warmly. "And you wrote a different ending—fierce loving."

She blinked, her eyes hot. "As much as I wanted you, the times we were together haunted me. It was so wrong. And then the night Brad shipped out, only one month after our wedding—"

"Nothing happened that night."

"Only because *you* stopped it." A tear escaped. "I used

you, Angel. I'm so ashamed of what I've done. And the night of the funeral—"

His mouth covered hers, silencing her. Not pushing for more, just sealing his mouth to hers long enough for her thoughts to still and her body to warm. He slid a hand into her hair, cupping her head, and broke the kiss, shifting to speak so close to her ear, she could feel as much as hear the words. "We were fast and furious that weekend back in college because the dam burst. You can only fight an attraction for so long. Those other times, you were vulnerable. You needed me close and I wanted to be close. But that's not where we're at now." He lifted his head to kiss her gently, tenderly in a way that reminded her of when he'd soothed her grief the night of the funeral, returning her weepy kisses with gentle tenderness. He pulled back and met her eyes. "I've never felt used. And nothing we've ever done was wrong."

"How can you say that?"

He rolled on top of her, his fingers entwining with hers, pushing their joined hands to the mattress on either side of her head. Her breathing ratcheted up as his thigh nudged hers apart, and he settled between her legs, bringing their bodies into full contact for the first time in ages. "Because of this. I know you feel it too. I can see it in your eyes."

"What do you see?" she asked softly.

"A deep connection of souls."

Her eyes filled, and she closed them, not wanting him to see so much. She'd chosen wrong. She'd used him, wanting to have it all, the wedding and the soul connection, holding both men to her when she should have let one of them go.

He kissed her tears away and then he kissed her, a coaxing kiss that she was helpless to resist. With every caress, every gentle urging, he seduced her into making love, forcing her to acknowledge it was more than a moment of wild abandon all those times she'd slept with him. Somehow he got them both naked while he kissed her, making her entire body sigh and melt into his. She ran her fingers through his soft hair as he moved to kiss her neck, sucking gently. A sob welled up. This was how Angel had been with her the night of Brad's funeral in this very bed, so gentle and tender, like he was trying to heal her with his body. Only it brought more shame and guilt crashing down over her then and now. Brad hadn't been in the grave for more than a day before she'd screwed Angel again. And then Angel had bailed when she needed him most.

She pushed at his chest.

Angel lifted his head. "What's wrong?"

"Get off. I can't do this."

He clenched his jaw. "Why?"

"Get off me!"

He rolled off her and stared at the ceiling. "Julia," he said slowly, "I've reached my limit. Seriously. Tell me why I can't have you right now or I'm gone."

Sure, bail on me again in the same damn bed!

She jackknifed up, so furious and hurt she didn't care that she was completely naked for this conversation. "You bailed on me."

He sat up too. "What? When?"

She spoke through her teeth. "After we fucked in my fucking marriage bed."

He stared at her mouth, and then he slowly traced her lips with one finger. She lost her train of thought, lost her breath. "When did you get such a dirty mouth?"

"When I met you."

"No-o," he said, dragging the word out like *try again*.

"When I fucked you. You're the dirty talker."

His hand slid into her hair, tugging enough to tilt her head for his kiss. She trembled. He leaned close and spoke against her mouth as his other hand unexpectedly slid between her legs, jolting her. "I know you want me, Julia. You're hot and wet." She watched as he took his finger, wet from her, lifted it to his mouth and sucked. Her lips parted, enthralled. He trailed his finger down her throat, his eyes hot on hers. "Now tell me why we can't fuck or we're done talking."

"I…" *Want this. Need this. Crave this.* It would be so easy to cave, but then what about after? She swallowed. "Angel."

His hand still cupped her head, tangled in her hair, holding her close. "I'm listening."

She closed her eyes and tried to focus. "You bailed on me, and I can't bear it if you bail again."

He dropped his hand. She opened her eyes to find him glaring at her. "I did not bail on you!" he barked. "I haven't left your side since the day we met! Ten fucking years!"

She scooted back, needing more space for this conversation. "The night of Brad's funeral. After we slept together, I woke up and you were gone. You didn't come back for a month. And then you were so distant."

He swallowed visibly. "You had a breakdown after you slept with me. I knew you weren't ready for us."

"I was grieving! I wasn't ready for anyone! But I still needed you."

His brows knit together. "I couldn't be with you and not touch you. Not after that."

She crossed her arms. "So you bailed."

"How about the way you bailed on me? You weren't married, weren't even engaged the first time we slept together. Then Brad's back on campus and it's so long Angel!"

"No. You disappeared."

"After you rushed to his side!"

She took a deep breath in and out. "We *were* engaged. How could I not go to the hospital?" Brad had landed in the hospital with severe dehydration the Monday after her weekend with Angel.

He scrubbed a hand over his face. "You slept with me when you were engaged to him? I thought it was just talk."

"It was understood. Our moms were already planning the wedding. So now you know how horrible a person I am! A big fat sinner! Cheating with my fiancé's best friend!"

They glared at each other for one long moment, the air practically sizzling with all the pent-up desire between them.

"Julia, this is happening," he said in a voice that brooked no argument.

"Yes." But it would happen on her terms.

His gaze raked over her, lingering on her sex. He reached out, his hand landing high on her upper thigh. Oh, no. They were not doing anything in this bed of bad memories. She scooted away and rolled out of bed.

"Get back here," Angel growled.

"Condoms are in my nightstand," she threw over her shoulder before strolling to the dresser. "Damon."

She heard the rustle of the condom wrapper.

"Who the hell were these for?" Angel demanded.

The box was new. She thought she might need them when she started dating again, but now she realized she'd been fooling herself.

"For you," she said simply.

And then his heat was at her back. He wrapped his arms around her, pinning her arms to her sides, and met her eyes in the mirror mounted over the dresser. "I remember this scene." His voice was rough and gravelly. "You want Damon?"

She didn't reply. His tone said he knew what they both needed.

He pushed her down over the dresser, shoved her legs apart, and pressed at her entrance, waiting. Her pulse thrummed in her ears, molten heat drenching her.

"Say it," he demanded. "Safe word or what you really crave."

She shivered, recognizing the words from her fantasy. "Take me."

He took her in one hard thrust. She cried out and then shuddered around him, her body already accepting what her mind wouldn't let her have. He snaked an arm around her, stroking her sweet spot as he pumped hard and fast, the way they both craved.

"Say my name," he ordered.

"Damon," she gasped out.

He didn't like that answer. He sank his teeth into the side of her neck and she clenched around him, hurtling toward release. He stopped stroking her and soothed her neck with his tongue, slowing things down. She made a tiny mewl of frustration.

"Why do you want Damon so much?" he asked, stroking lightly as he pulled nearly all the way out and then slammed back in.

Her breath hitched. He stilled, deep inside her, so she told him exactly why. "Damon doesn't bail! The lines are clear. Fuck and release. Fuck again."

"That mouth," he groaned, sliding his finger across her bottom lip and then pushing it into her mouth. She sucked, tasting her desire for him. She spread her legs wider and lifted her hips. He rocked into her, hitting just the right spot, making her legs quiver as waves of pleasure coursed through her. He pulled her up off the dresser just enough to stroke his fingers down her throat, sliding further down to cup her breast and then pinch her nipple. She arched her back, pleasure radiating through her, her insides tightening around him. His hand slid between her legs, controlling her with firm strokes as his other hand held her hip, keeping her in place for a slow screw. She panted, lost in a haze of pleasure.

"Open your eyes," he rasped.

She did and their eyes met in the mirror. His were startlingly fierce.

"I'm going to break you," he growled.

She closed her eyes, shutting him out. "I'm already broken."

"Not the way I want. Not the way you need." His fingers were wicked, stroking her the way that made her crazed, drawing out whimpers of need. "Every wall is coming—"

She cried out as her release hit with shocking force. The word "coming" from his lips was all she needed to send her over the edge. She shuddered and sank down, resting her cheek on the dresser.

"More," he growled, grabbing her and yanking her back onto him. She lifted her head, gasping as he cupped her sex in a firm hold while he pumped, each thrust pushing her open onto his firm fingers, jolting and electrifying her until there was nothing but this incredible sensation of possession as he took and gave, pushing her higher and higher. Her knees buckled, but he had her tight, urging her on as he told her in explicit detail what he wanted from her, what she'd come to crave. She broke, the room dimming as she soared. He pumped into her, bringing intense aftershocks before his own release. Finally he stilled.

She couldn't move, locked in his hold; she caught her breath, her heart still pounding. His breath rasped near her ear. He wouldn't bail on her now. He couldn't because Damon always returned for more. He eased off her, and she stayed in position, limp and sated, across the dresser top. This was better than the bed. No bad memories.

He scooped her up and carried her back to bed. She was so relaxed, her eyes were already drifting closed. He lay next to her, his heat lulling her into sleep.

"Stay," she mumbled before drifting off.

When she woke a short while later, he was gone.

She sat up. "Angel?"

No answer.

People bailed on her—her mother, Brad, even Angel—but she thought this time was different. She thought Damon would be different. And, for the first time, instead of feeling helpless and sad over being left behind, she felt only fury.

She spotted a note on the nightstand: *This isn't bailing. I need some space to think about us.*

Argh! Saying you weren't bailing didn't mean you weren't! Damon didn't need space, didn't need to think! She shredded that stupid note until it was tiny specks of lie. Then she grabbed her cell and texted him one word—taradiddle. Both because she wanted his hands off and because he was a damned liar. He *did* bail. If he had to think about them so much, he should've done it with her so they could talk.

She tossed the phone on the nightstand, grabbed a pillow, and gave it a knockout punch.

13

Angel showed up to Sunday family dinner after his tumul-
tuous night and morning with Julia, doing his best to stay
upbeat. Everyone was talking about Luke and Kennedy's
wedding on Saturday. The bachelor party was Thursday
night, rehearsal Friday night. Angel, along with his brothers
and Kennedy's brothers—five in all—would be groomsmen.
His older brother Nico was best man. And only two days
later, he'd be a groomsman in Ally's wedding. All this
wedding business was pissing him off. He pushed some potatoes around on his plate. Why did everyone else get to find
their forever love and acknowledge it in front of God and
man, and he had to channel his dark side to get only part of
what he wanted from Julia? And her text meant to keep his
hands off just pissed him off more. No safe word in the world
was going to put that genie back in the bottle. They'd crossed
the line of no return, and he'd waited too long to have her to
go back now.

The problem was he'd felt empty after they made love.
Well, it was more like fucking than making love. She'd
surrendered her body to Damon. But Angel wanted it all—
body, heart, and soul. He'd left, needing a long drive to figure
out how to move things to where they felt right.

He stabbed a potato and shoved it in his mouth. He

couldn't believe she accused him of bailing when she was the one who bailed on him! Of course he hadn't stuck around after she had a freaking breakdown the last time they'd slept together. Her sobbing grief had chilled him. He knew she needed to grieve, not get tangled up in him. Besides, he'd called. That should count, right?

A niggling of doubt tugged at him. She had abandonment issues from being adopted and him bailing after Brad had bailed (through no fault of his own) must've been extra difficult. She'd needed him, and he wasn't there. Plain and simple. But he was only human, distance was the only way he could think of to keep his hands to himself after their explosive hookup. He'd done the best he could at the time, but now he was starting to see it differently.

He flashed back to the first time they hooked up back in college. He'd made himself scarce, believing she'd made her choice when she rushed to Brad's side at the hospital. He couldn't bear to see them together after that weekend. But seeing it now through Julia's eyes, all she'd known was that when she got back to campus, he was gone. He'd rejoined their little group a month later. He'd missed her too much to stay away.

He stifled a groan as the truth hit him—he'd backed off when he should've stepped up. That first time Brad asked her out, Angel should've told her how he felt instead of biding his time for months, waiting for Brad to get tired of her. And then, when he and Julia finally did give in to temptation, after a year of friendship, he should've stuck around and fought for her. That had been a mistake, covering it up. Because then Julia suffered with guilt, and Brad had been wronged, and Angel still couldn't be with the woman he loved. The whole thing had snowballed after that—his hurt keeping him at a distance, Julia's guilt and worry over Brad shipping out, Brad's oblivious plan for a wedding before he left for boot camp.

Nearly two years of missed opportunities, missteps, mistakes. And then she was married, and Angel wouldn't cross that line. The marriage vows were sacred to him. He'd stopped the one time he and Julia had drawn together the night Brad shipped out because she was married.

They needed a damned do-over for their entire fucked-up relationship.

Couldn't she see by now that they kept coming together because they were soul mates? They were drawn together, made for each other, and even Brad with his preemptive move on Julia way back when couldn't break that bond.

He blinked, refocusing on his family, all of them deep in conversation about wedding food. Kennedy had ordered a huge tiered wedding cake, along with a dessert buffet of pastries and, of course, his stepmom's Italian wedding cookies. Ironic because the first time Kennedy had eaten the delicious crescent-shaped wedding cookies covered in powdered sugar that somehow caused rapid-fire marriage proposals to spout from his brothers, she'd spit them out. Now she considered them sacred. Everyone was teasing her about them, especially Luke.

"Those cookies are magic," Luke said, widening his blue eyes and wiggling his fingers in the air. "One bite and Kennedy got in line lickety-split."

"Not quite, Reynolds," Kennedy replied. She was a petite, blond fireball that gave as good as she got.

Everyone laughed, even Angel got a kick out of their banter. Luke had truly met his match. Too bad Angel had met his too soon. He was beginning to think everything about relationships was in the timing.

"Did you invite Julia to the wedding?" Emily asked Angel.

He gazed at her for a long moment, lost in thought, remembering Julia's earlier confession about why she wrote the Fierce trilogy. Emily had been the girlfriend that kicked Julia into a fit of jealous erotic romance writing. His twisted life just got even more twisted. He suddenly realized the room was silent. Quite a feat around the crowded dining room table with his dad, his stepmom, five newly domesticated brothers, five close-knit opinionated sisters-in-law, and a toddler.

Angel flashed a grin, trying for a joking manner. "I thought maybe Dad put the kibosh on that name."

"I did, son," his dad replied. "I wanted you to have time to step up or step off after your date without any comments from the peanut gallery, but it's been more than a month." He looked at him, silently waiting for Angel to fill in the blank.

"I stepped up," Angel said.

Everyone cheered. Angel shook his head, smiling. "Thank you, but it's complicated." He looked around the table at the people he loved, who he knew meant well, but he couldn't explain all the twisted history between him and Julia. "We're not there yet."

"Bring her to the wedding," Kennedy ordered. He hesitated to call her bridezilla, she was too soft-hearted for that, but she'd certainly made sure everything was perfect for her special day. Kennedy leaned across the table toward him, her expression fierce. "Make her eat a cookie. Don't tell her why. The rest will take care of itself."

Luke barked out a laugh at Kennedy's side.

Kennedy turned and glared at him.

Luke kissed her soundly on the mouth. "I love you, babe." He held her by the chin and gazed into her eyes. "Love, love, love." Kennedy blinked rapidly, and Luke pulled her close, tucking her head against his chest.

Angel caught Jared's eye, his brother's expression radiating concern and maybe a little pity. He'd always been closest to Jared, ever since they'd been thrown together at eight years old to share parents, a room, and a classroom. They were both easygoing enough to make the sudden transition work.

Angel stared at his plate for a moment and then abruptly stood. "I'll get the dishes. You all go ahead and finalize the wedding stuff."

Conversation resumed as Kennedy suddenly remembered the dyed color of the bridesmaids' shoes wasn't quite right and wondered if they had time for the women to all go shoe shopping. Angel gathered as many plates as he could hold and headed to the adjoining kitchen. Jared joined him a moment later with another stack of plates.

"How can I help?" Jared asked. He meant with Julia. Jared hated kitchen duty.

"I got it." He ran some water over the dishes.

But Jared wasn't so easily put off. "Ask me anything and I'll do it. I never would've gotten through to Emily without all your feelings talk."

Angel's throat got tight. He shut off the water. "Jare."

"I mean it."

He met his stepbrother's green eyes. "You would've figured it out."

Jared socked him on the shoulder. "I'll get Emily in on it if you think it'll help. Maybe it's a chick thing."

"No!" Angel blurted. Geez, that would be a disaster, what with Emily being his ex and the Fierce trilogy that resulted from that relationship. He suddenly remembered Julia's casual mention of how she'd written the books because *her vibrator* wasn't doing it for her. There wasn't much Julia could say to surprise him after all these years, but that had been news to him. If he didn't want her so much himself, he would've asked her for a demonstration with it. He probably could've coaxed her into it too because, after all these years, her trust in him was absolute. So why couldn't she trust him with her heart?

Yes, mistakes were made, by both of them, but that was in the past. There had to be a way for them to move forward together. He just wasn't sure how to do that.

"Double date?" Jared asked.

"It's more of a feelings-talk thing," Angel said. "My specialty."

Jared inclined his head. "All right, then do your thing."

He gritted his teeth. "I'm trying."

Jared gave him a silent look of commiseration, the kind he was so good at with his doctor training. Angel struggled for the words to explain the problem without giving away Julia's secrets.

"It's like she needs absolution from her sins," Angel finally said.

Jared's green eyes widened. "Wait a minute. Are we talking about the same girl-next-door, first-grade teacher widow? *She's* a sinner?"

Don't forget erotic romance author.

Angel jerked his chin.

"Give her absolution, then. You're Saint Angel."

Angel shoved Jared. "Fuck you." He was so sick of his brothers calling him a saint or a priest. He was just as much a sinner as Julia was, though he felt zero guilt for taking what he wanted. He'd told her before, and he believed it with all his heart, nothing they'd ever done together was wrong. Yes, the circumstances could've been better, but nothing changed the fact that they belonged together.

"He's our resident priest, all right," his older brother Vince said, setting a stack of plates on the counter next to the sink. He was a big wisecracking guy with a mushy heart.

Angel glared at Vince. "Shut up."

Vince shoved Angel's head and then ruffled his hair. "You're the last bachelor we got."

"I know it," Angel said, "believe me."

Jared and Vince, on either side of Angel, exchanged a look. They spoke at the same time. "I'll fix this."

Angel blew out a breath. Sometimes being the youngest really sucked. Jared was only two months older, but he'd always claimed big brother status. His brothers had looked out for him as a kid, but that wouldn't work now. "There's nothing you can do."

Vince rubbed the back of his neck, peeked into the dining room where the talk was still rapid-fire over wedding details, and looked back to Angel. "Maybe you should get a real priest. Soph brought Father Munson into the conversation about Mom, and it did help." Vince had apparently harbored guilt over not visiting their mother's grave.

"Yeah," Jared chimed in from Angel's other side. "Maybe she just needs to go to confession."

Angel couldn't imagine Julia confessing to a priest what

they'd done let alone explaining the Fierce trilogy. "I'll be her confessor."

"Oh-hoo-hoo!" Vince chortled. "What kind of penance are we talking?"

Jared grinned. "Well, she's got to be on her knees."

"You're both going to hell," Angel said with a wide grin.

Jared hip-checked Angel, bumping him into Vince. "We'll see you there."

Angel went to work at his usual early time Monday morning, settled into his private office, and booted up his laptop. He liked to review his schedule and notes before the students arrived so he could be available at a moment's notice if needed. He'd just picked up his cup of coffee when Julia strode in, startling him. She never showed up early for work. He set the mug back down. She was wearing the dark blue sweater that clung to her breasts and a skirt with bare legs in flats. He would've preferred heels, but it *was* work. She'd be on her feet all day in the classroom. His mind wandered to what she had on under the skirt when he realized she was eerily silent.

He met her dark blue eyes for the first time and discovered she was glaring like a would-be murderess. He'd be lying if he said it didn't do something for him. She was more a preemptive apologizer than a fighter. The fire in her eyes was captivating.

"Good morning," he said, by which he meant *good glory, gimme some of that.*

She shut the door behind her and locked it. He watched in fascination, all of this unprecedented in their shared history of working at Eastman Elementary. Her hands were in fists and she closed the distance between them. She lifted a hand over his desk and sprinkled it with white confetti.

"Just because you say you're not bailing," she snapped, "doesn't mean you didn't actually bail."

He glanced at the confetti again, saw ink marks and realized it was his note. "Nice," he muttered. "Look—"

"No, you look!" Her eyes flashed, igniting him. He loved that she was fiery instead of sad or hurt. "I hope you got the meaning of that text I sent that you *ignored*. Just like you ignored me." She smacked her palms flat on the desk and got in his face. "Hands off from now on."

"Sorry," he replied calmly, "your safe word expired when I bent you over the dresser, spread your legs, and fu—"

She raised a hand to slap him, and he caught her wrist before she made contact. She struggled to get free, and he tightened his grip, watching her cheeks and neck rise with color. Damn, she was making him hot, and this was really not the place.

"Let's dance," he said.

She stopped struggling and stared at him blankly, probably because they never danced, which gave him enough time to maneuver around the desk to where she stood. He wrapped an arm around her waist. "Hey, darling." He backed her slowly toward the closed door like a dance that had them walking together, pelvis to pelvis.

"I'm not your darling," she snapped. "And we're not dancing."

"We kinda are," he said.

Her back hit the door and he boxed her in, his hands on either side of her head, all up in her space. Her eyes flashed, making him rock hard.

"Damon doesn't bail," she said in a voice filled with annoyance. Like he'd missed the most important point in the Damon-Mia experience.

That was when it hit him how to make things right. This was the classic two birds with one flying fuck. He wouldn't have to stop sleeping with her, and he'd eventually get them from *Fierce Craving* to *Fierce Loving*. He'd play out her fantasies all the way through Mia and Damon's true love happy ending. Damon even proposed at the end, and Mia happily accepted. That was also her secret desire. With him.

He watched her as he slowly shifted position, cupping her

shoulders and then sliding his hands down her arms. "What does Damon do instead of bail?" He knew but he loved hearing her say out loud her secret desires.

"Fuck and release and fuck again." She narrowed her eyes. "He always promises to return."

He squeezed her hand and slid his other hand to her bare knee, lifting the edge of her skirt. "But he doesn't spend the night, does he?" He slowly slid his hand further up, along her soft inner thigh, waiting for her to stop him. The staff and students would arrive soon.

But she didn't stop him. Instead her eyes softened, and she licked her lips. He reached her panties and drew his finger across the damp cotton panel. She shivered. He pushed the panties out of the way and slid a finger inside her, drawing a soft moan. He drew back and slid another finger in as he spoke near her ear. "I will be your Damon, and I promise to return." He stroked her hard nub with his thumb as he thrust inside with his fingers.

"Yes," she hissed. He didn't know if she was agreeing to the fantasy or just loving his hand up her skirt, but it didn't matter because he was going to do both. He shifted his hand, pressing up on the inside to stroke her G-spot as he ground the heel of his hand right on her *oh-more* spot. Her soft sounds of pleasure made him thicker and harder. She was fever-hot, soaking his fingers, clenching and unclenching around him.

"Every night," he told her as he stroked and ground and she clutched his shirt. "Every erotic scene in those books."

"Promise," she gasped out.

"Fuck and release—"

She cried out, shuddering with her release, and he covered the sound with his mouth on hers. He stroked some more, swallowing her sexy cries as she rode every last wave of pleasure. She finally stilled, and he slid his hand away, watching to see what she'd do next. Her cheeks and neck were flushed pink. She didn't seem mad anymore.

She straightened her skirt and shot him a wary look.

He cupped her cheek and kissed her tenderly. "Good little Mia. I'll return for you tonight. And every night. Promise."

Her dark blue eyes lit up. "I won't use my safe word."

He grinned. "You don't have a safe word."

She shivered, gave him a small, sexy smile and sailed out the door.

Now that was a plan. A good plan. He headed outside for a brisk walk while he thought about superintendent meetings and other crap that would surely make his pants more comfortable.

~

Angel kept his promise. Every night he went to Julia's place and made her every fantasy come true—in a wide variety of places—the bath, the wall, the bed (only non-missionary position), the chair, the counter, bent over the sofa…damn, that woman had a good imagination. Except they couldn't do the dining room table scene. She didn't have one. He'd tried to get her to his place, where a dining room table was conveniently waiting, but she resisted, and when he pushed, she distracted him by dropping to her knees and unzipping his pants. *Fuck me*, there was nothing hotter than watching her sweet mouth take him in.

But now it was Thursday night, and he had to go to Luke's bachelor party. Nico had reserved the back room of Lombardi's, an Italian restaurant in Eastman his family liked. Angel helped himself to a beer at the open bar and took a seat next to Jared at one of the round tables surrounding a small cleared area of floor.

"What's the entertainment?" Angel asked. Luke had invited his wealthy friends, including his biggest client, Bentley Williams, so he really hoped Nico had bypassed strippers. Angel always worried about strippers and ended up talking to them about an alternate vocation. They were often single moms, and he had a lot of contacts in local government agencies and nonprofit organizations that could help.

"You'll see," Jared said, taking a long pull on his beer.

"What, is it a secret?"

Just then tiny tinkling bells rang out and a group of

women strolled in wearing sequined gold bikini-style tops and gold and black harem pants.

Jared grinned. "Belly dancers. Lily found them." That was Nico's wife.

The women set up their music and one of them set a chair in the center of the cleared area. A woman with long wavy black hair and a heavily made-up face scanned the room. "The groom?"

"Lu-u-ke!" Nico bellowed through cupped hands, though Luke wasn't far away.

Luke held up a hand, grinning, before taking the seat in the center. The music began and the women began a sensuous harem-style dance around Luke, their tiny finger cymbals and bells around their wrists and ankles chiming in a pleasant beat. Everyone was hooting and hollering.

He glanced around the room at his brothers, Luke's friends, even his dad, spellbound by the intricate dance. Not him. Julia ruined him for other women, and he was still nowhere near the happy ending marriage proposal part. He hated to admit it because he was enjoying the hell out of being her fantasy, but things still weren't right. She didn't want to look at him when they screwed. Still wanted him behind her. He had to make her look at him, make her face him, and then she got mad, but they still fucked anyway because a fiery Julia turned him on even more. Honestly, everything she did turned him on now that he knew he could have her naked whenever he wanted.

He took a long pull on his beer. He'd reread the ending of *Fierce Loving*, and it wasn't clear what made Mia face Damon finally in the light. The author hadn't explained that part to his satisfaction.

Maybe he should've invited her to Luke's wedding like Kennedy said and make her eat the Italian wedding cookies. He'd avoided it because the last time he'd seen Julia at a wedding had been her own, and he'd about died that day. Of course, they had Ally's wedding to get through anyway, so why not pile on another wedding? Why not try his step-mom's way? He'd get Julia to the wedding, make her eat a cookie, and wait for the magic. It was pathetic and ridiculous and he was just desperate enough to try.

Besides, it was time she got to know his family. That was where this thing between them was heading. She would be part of his family soon if he had anything to say about it. And he did.

He pulled out his cell and texted her. *What are you doing Saturday?*

Ally's bachelorette party.

He bristled. It didn't matter that he was currently at a bachelor party, drinking and watching half-naked women writhing on the dance floor. He didn't want her doing the same. Would she be ogling male strippers? Pretending *they* were Damon? *Forget all that. Stay focused.*

He texted again. *Strippers?*

You know Ally.

So yes. He gritted his teeth. *What time?*

Why? You going to join us?

Maybe I will.

Just us girls.

Can you—he stopped. Deleted that. *Will you*—delete. He rubbed his forehead. This was absurd. He was supposed to be able to handle emotionally charged situations.

He tried again for a carefully neutral tone. *How do you feel about going to Luke's wedding? Saturday at noon.* He figured Ally's bachelorette party was probably at night.

She didn't reply. Maybe he should've done this in person. He'd go to her place right after this. But what if they just ended up fucking again? He shifted uncomfortably. Not that he minded fucking Julia, but at some point it was going to blow up in his face. His cell vibrated, and he glanced down.

Are you sure the bride doesn't mind a last-minute guest?

He was so relieved he felt light-headed for a moment. *She insists.*

Why would the bride insist? I've never met her.

I'm the only single guy in the wedding party.

Am I your date?

Do you want to be?

No answer. He grabbed his leather jacket and headed outside for more privacy. The texting wasn't doing it. He had to hear her voice. His cell vibrated with a return text.

I miss you.

He pressed her number on speed dial and walked further away from the restaurant. "I miss you too," he said as soon as she answered. It was the first night they'd been apart since their Damon-Mia reunion three days ago.

"Why do you want me at the wedding all of a sudden?" she asked.

He blew out a breath. "Maybe we should talk face to face."

"You're too tempting face to face."

He found himself smiling. "Yeah?"

"You really have to ask? I nearly lost consciousness with that last orgasm."

He groaned.

"And I wrote three books about our one weekend in bed."

His chest puffed out. "So you did."

"Can you talk now?"

"I'm at Luke's bachelor party. I'll stop by after. This is too important for the phone."

"Fine, but no Damon. I *will* use my safe word."

"I thought we did away with that." He chuckled. "Okay, let me hear it."

"Tara—" She giggled. He grinned. He loved hearing that carefree giggle. "I can't say it. It's ridiculous."

"That's exactly why I picked it. Also the hidden meaning." It was a small hint that he was onto the secret desires she denied. A liar to her own body.

"How far would you go?" she asked eagerly. "Would you push me to my limits? Would you truly break me?"

He went rock hard. Fuck. She would let him do anything. She *wanted* him to do anything. Holy hell.

"Angel?"

"Yeah," he managed.

"Can you come over like right now?"

He shoved a hand in his hair. How did this conversation get away from him? They were supposed to be talking about them and their future, not having phone sex. He had to get things back on track.

He lowered his voice. "Get out your vibrator, let me hear you come, and then I'll be there for a serious talk."

She moaned, making him harder. "But Bob the third isn't as good as you."

He choked on a laugh. Bob the third? "You have three vibrators named Bob?"

"No, just one. The first two Bobs wore out."

He barked out a laugh. He had no idea she was such a horny thing all these years. They could've been fucking a lot more than they had. Any sign from her, the smallest thing, and he would've been all over her.

"It's not funny," she said. "It's been very difficult to deal with everything."

He got serious. "I could've helped you out before you got to Bob the third. What took you so damn long?"

"You were my forbidden fruit," she said softly.

Guilt and sin. Yeah, he could see that. "And now?"

She sighed. "You said it yourself, the genie's out of the bottle."

He found himself smiling. "Can't put him back, can we?"

"Her. And no. She's a demanding bitch."

He slowly shook his head, loving hearing more spirit in her voice. For so long, she'd been a faint wisp of the Julia he knew and loved.

She spoke again, this time in a tempting seductress voice that grabbed him by the balls. "Do you remember what Damon—"

"I'll stop by in a couple hours," he said through clenched teeth. "To talk."

"I like your voice on the phone," she went on silkily. She knew what she was doing to him. "It's so *deep* and sexy."

He groaned. "Goodbye, Julia."

"Deep, deeper, *ooh, yes,* deeper."

"I said goodbye!" he exclaimed with mock anger.

She giggled. "Bye."

Angel hung up, did a few brisk trips around the block in

the cold winter air to cool down, and headed back inside just as the belly dancers were leaving, chattering happily. His oldest stepbrother, Gabe, got a few tables going with poker, and some guys were playing pool in the adjoining area.

Luke thumped Angel on the back. "Hey, where'd you get off to? You missed the belly finale." He did a comical hip wiggle to demonstrate.

Angel chuckled. "I had a phone call. Julia's coming to the wedding on Saturday."

"Yeah? Hey, that's great. Kennedy will be thrilled. Be careful though. If you don't get Julia to the cookies, Kennedy will bring the cookies to her. Probably shove them down her gullet. She loves you, that's all."

"Who?"

"Kennedy, who you think?"

For a moment he thought Luke meant Julia. But he wouldn't know that. He'd only met her a couple of times. Once over the summer when she and Brad stopped by. Once after the funeral. Did Julia love him? It occurred to him that she'd never said the words. Of course, neither had he, and he definitely did love her. She had to know that, right?

"So things are better with you two?" Luke asked.

"Getting there."

"Ah, women," Luke said, shaking his head. "Such a pain in our—" He stiffened and pulled his cell out of his pants pocket. It must've been on vibrate. "Hey, beautiful," he cooed into the phone. "I miss you so much." He strode off, murmuring, "I miss you more."

Man, his brothers were so whipped.

Angel showed up at Julia's house only one hour later, purposely losing at poker to make his escape. He knocked, but there was no answer. It was eleven o'clock on a work night. Had she fallen asleep? He had to see her. This talk couldn't wait any longer. He knocked again, a little harder. Had she used the vibrator? She often fell asleep after she came because it relaxed her so much. That was it. He pulled out his key and let himself in. The place was dark. He locked the door behind him and headed toward her bedroom.

She was sleeping diagonally across the center of the bed, taking up all the space. He gazed at her for a moment in the dim moonlight peeking through the blinds. Her dark hair was in wild disarray, her soft lips parted slightly. How he longed to just strip down and curl up in bed beside her, but something stopped him. Lying in bed with Julia never led to talking.

Instead he leaned over, brushed her hair back and kissed her temple. Then using what little willpower he had left, he turned and walked out the door.

14

Angel stood in line with the groomsmen at the front of St. Joseph's, the Catholic church in Clover Park, for Luke's wedding with a strong sense of the familiar. It wasn't that long ago he'd stood up here for Vince and Sophia's wedding. He caught Julia's eye where she sat next to Emily in the row with his sisters-in-law. She gave him a tight smile. She warmed up slowly to people, so he really hoped that meant she wouldn't be exchanging confidences with Emily any time soon. Like how Emily was his ex-girlfriend, the same one that made Julia jealous enough to pen the Fierce trilogy. Emily had remembered Julia from a cooking class they'd taken back in December and had been chatting her up ever since they arrived. Angel never talked about anyone he dated by name to Julia and, likewise, never mentioned Julia by name to a girlfriend. Some part of him knew deep down that any woman would come in second place to Julia.

He planned on driving Julia to the reception in Greenport, instead of riding in the limo, so they'd get a chance to talk. It was a half-hour drive to the beachside estate of Luke's client and close friend Bentley, so that should be enough time to get a few things straight. The music began, and the bridesmaids started their slow walk down the aisle. Kennedy's younger sisters, Frank and Jamie, went first followed by Kennedy's friends Hailey (from book club, apparently they grew up together), another friend he didn't know, and the matron of honor, Candy (Bentley's wife). Hailey had wanted to plan Kennedy's wedding and have it at Ludbury House where she worked, but Kennedy wanted the church wedding and the estate reception. They'd had a catered rehearsal dinner at Ludbury House last night for just the bridal party as a compromise.

Finally, the bridesmaids and matron of honor were in place, and the traditional "Here Comes the Bride" song began. Kennedy appeared in a white satin gown with a long train. She wore no veil, only a thin diamond headband in her blond hair done up in a twist. Intricate lace decorated the top of the sleeveless dress, matching her lace gloves. He knew the dress was designer, there'd been a lot of excitement over it among the women in the family, and he had to admit, she was stunning. Her dad stood next to her, standing stiffly since he was still recovering from back surgery.

Kennedy practically glided down the aisle, a small smile playing over her lips. Angel glanced at Luke, who was beaming. By the time Kennedy got to Luke, she was also beaming.

Father Munson began the ceremony, a traditional service that gave Angel plenty of time to remember Julia's wedding, with him standing as witness, the best man dying on the inside. It had been so hard not to let his true feelings show in his expression, especially because Julia kept her gaze fixed on him for most of the ceremony. He'd at first thought it was because she wanted him instead of Brad, but later when he asked her about it at the reception, she said if she focused on him, she could forget everyone was looking at her. He'd wanted to know why looking at Brad didn't do the same thing for her, but then Brad swooped in and led her to the dance floor.

He never did find out why.

Now, he slid a look over to Julia, who had a pleasant expression pasted on her face, but he knew her well enough to know weddings weren't much easier for her. She must be remembering Brad and missing him.

Finally, Father Munson announced, "You may kiss the bride."

Luke gazed at Kennedy, cupped her face in both hands and kissed her reverently. When he pulled back, the crowd erupted in applause, but Luke didn't seem to notice. He just stood there, cupping his new wife's face, gazing adoringly. Kennedy burst into happy tears. That set off a chain reaction with his stepmom, his dad, and Vince, the softies in the family. Angel's throat was tight, half in reaction to their happiness, half for his own sadness over still not having Julia as his own.

Kennedy and Luke headed down the aisle, hand in hand, smiling, followed by their entourage of bridesmaids and groomsmen. He looked over at Julia on his way down the aisle, who gave him a small smile. All of his sisters-in-law in the row with her were wiping tears.

After saying his congratulations to the happy couple along with his family, Angel found Julia waiting by his car. She wore a blue dress with swirls on it that hugged her curves. It had tiny sleeves and showed lots of skin. A small white wrap over her arms added little warmth. He wanted nothing more than to run his hands down her sides, feeling the gentle curve in at the waist and over the slope of her hip. Instead he did the gentlemanly thing and unlocked the car, ushering her in so she wouldn't get too cold. It wasn't a biting cold, but February in Connecticut was still chilly.

"It was a really nice wedding," she said once he got in the car. "So that's everyone, right? All your brothers are married?"

He started the car. "One more. Jared gets married in June."

"And then that's everyone."

"Yup." He pulled out of the lot and followed the line of cars out to Main Street before adding, "Everyone but me."

She turned on the radio. "Kennedy looked so beautiful. Exactly like a bride should look on her wedding day."

"Yes. You look beautiful too." He stole a peek at her legs where the dress had ridden up high.

"Aww...thank you." She tugged her dress down. "This is my bridesmaid dress for Ally's wedding, so you'll see me in it again in two days."

A silence fell. Finally when he got to a red light, he decided just to dive into the murky emotional mess between them.

"Julia," he said at the same time she said, "Angel."

"Sorry, you go ahead," he said.

"You looked sad at the wedding," she said.

"So did you."

"Weddings are hard for me."

"Because you miss Brad?" he asked.

"No."

He waited in silence. One of the first things they taught him as a social worker was to quietly listen.

"I just remember my wedding," she finally said. "How nervous I was. Remember?"

He didn't. His own gut had been churning, coloring everything through a haze of envy. He only remembered how nervous Brad was. He'd been in the back room of the church with Brad. Julia had been tucked behind closed doors by the entrance of the church so Brad wouldn't see her gown before the wedding. "Did you have cold feet?"

"Yes."

He stared straight ahead. What was she trying to tell him? Did she have doubts? Or maybe it was just her natural shyness that made being the center of attention uncomfortable for her.

"The light's green," she said.

He blinked and hit the gas. "Julia," he said slowly, "did you have doubts about marrying Brad, or was it just nerves?"

"Both," she said softly.

His heart squeezed painfully. "Why did you go through with it?"

She blew out a breath. "Brad needed to be married before

he went off to a war zone. He needed something to come home to."

That hit him like a slap. He pulled over to a quiet side street and parked. He turned to her and watched her expression. "So you married Brad for your duty?"

She wrung her hands together and looked away.

"Julia!" he said half angry, half desperate.

Her head jerked up. "I married Brad for the same reason you agreed to be his best man, even though you didn't want me marrying him." He'd never said that in so many words, but she'd gotten the message. "Because we loved him."

Red-hot rage surged through him. All the wasted years. All the hurt and grief and loss. "Dammit, Julia! Your wedding was the most painful day of my life!"

"It's too late now!" she exclaimed before adding, "I'm sorry."

He instantly regretted lashing out at her. Had they both gone into that wedding out of a misplaced sense of duty for their best friend?

His voice came out hoarse. "I just can't believe I'm hearing this now after all these years."

She shook her head. "You can't undo the past. It's too late."

He grabbed her by the shoulders. "It's not too late. I refuse to believe that."

"Tell me how to fix this and I will!" she cried.

"I don't know! If I knew, I would've fixed it five years ago!"

The look in her eyes pained him—hurt and angry and hopeless. He dropped his hands from her, cursing himself for losing his temper. He was trained for this, for dealing with volatile emotional situations. Why couldn't he use his social worker skills with her? It was just too close, too painful to have any kind of professional distance.

He wrapped her in a hug, and she rested her head on his chest.

"I don't want to hurt you." She sighed. "And I'm tired of hurting."

And then he knew what they needed to do—forgive. It was the only way to put the past behind them.

"You need to forgive Brad," he told her, "for lying to you about the adoption. And then you need to forgive yourself for being with me when you were still with him." *And I need to forgive you for leaving me behind,* he added silently.

She pulled away and scowled. "I can't forgive Brad. He ruined everything. And you—" she jabbed a finger in his chest "—I can't pretend it was just the heat of the moment when I spent the entire weekend screwing you. What I did was wrong, and I can't forgive myself for that. Brad ended up in the hospital while I was cheating on him."

"I spent that weekend making love not screwing."

She threw her hands up. "Same thing!"

"It's not!"

They stared at each other, at an impasse, so he did the only thing he knew would work. He cupped her neck and pulled her in for a hard kiss, the rough kind that she couldn't help but respond to, the kind that said this was a lust that could not be denied. And when she melted against him, he pulled away.

He put the car in gear and pulled back onto the main road, heading to the reception.

"What's happening to us?" she asked. "Are we—should we try to go back to being friends?"

Impossible. "Nope. We're going to screw some more. You might as well take off your panties now. As soon as you get a chance, you're going into the ladies' room at the reception, and I'm going to bend you over and fuck you."

As if he'd said the most flowery loving words instead of the crudest, she lit up with a smile and wiggled around in her seat, slipping off her panties and holding up the tiny scrap of pink silk to show him before stuffing them in her purse. He wanted to bang his head against the steering wheel in frustration, but his body wouldn't be denied. He'd been hands off for too long to do anything but take what she offered.

Julia wasn't in the wedding party, so for the first part of the reception she couldn't sit with Angel, who was at a long table of bridal party people for all the early stuff. It was a sit-down meal and she found herself at a table with some of Angel's sisters-in-law—Emily, Sophia, Lily, and Zoe. Sophia, Lily, and Zoe were deep in conversation about their pregnancies (Zoe wasn't pregnant, but she had experience that the other two were eating up). There were some squicky details that Julia tried her best not to overhear. Emily traded seats with Sophia to sit next to Julia.

"We'll have our own nonpregnant conversation over here," Emily said with a smile. She was Jared's fiancée. She and Emily resembled each other a bit, nearly the same height and build, both of them with straight shoulder-length dark brown hair, the fair skin of the Irish, though Emily's eyes were brown not blue like hers. She'd been super nice ever since Julia arrived. She'd chatted with her a few months ago too at the cooking classes she'd taken with Angel.

"Sounds good," Julia whispered, not wanting to offend the other women, who were extremely enthusiastic in their oversharing.

"Beautiful wedding, wasn't it?" Emily asked.

"Absolutely. I loved her gown."

"Kennedy's friend Candy knows all the best designers. Mucho money." Emily rubbed her fingers together. The tuxedoed waiter arrived with their food. They enjoyed Cornish hen, roasted potatoes, and French beans while Emily filled Julia in on her own wedding planning. Julia just smiled and nodded, knowing next to nothing about planning a wedding.

They finished their meal and Emily put a hand on her arm. "You're such a good listener, I'm afraid I just went on and on."

"No, it's fine," Julia said. "It's nice. I mean, I'm happy for you."

Emily beamed. "And I'm so happy to see you here with Angel. Aww, he's looking at you."

Julia met Angel's eye, and he winked. She wiggled her fingers at him.

Emily gave him an enthusiastic wave before turning back to Julia. "He's so fun. Great guy."

"Yeah. He's been my best friend for ten years."

"But he's more than that now, right? You're together?"

Julia flushed. It was so hard to explain without sharing too much. "I don't know. It's complicated."

Emily snorted. "Complicated, I get, believe me." She lowered her voice and leaned close. "I've gotta say the moment I saw you two at cooking class—the way he looks at you, the way you look at him, it's obvious the love between you."

Julia clasped her hands tightly together and stared at the table. "We've always been close."

"I don't mean close like friends. When I saw the way he looked at you, I was glad he let me go. I knew his love for you was so strong he never would've had room in his heart for me."

Julia's head snapped around. "What do you mean let you go? I thought you were with Jared."

Emily's brown eyes went wide. "I am." She cringed. "I am so sorry. He never mentioned me by name, did he?" She shook her head. "Of course he didn't, he never mentioned you by name either. I just knew as soon as I saw you together."

Julia's hands went clammy even as she felt her cheeks burning. She didn't like this one bit. Why would Angel put her in this position? Leave her to walk right into a hugely embarrassing situation, sitting and chatting with his ex-lover. She glared at Angel, who didn't notice because he was busy talking to Jared.

Emily put a hand on her arm. "I'm so sorry! I can see I surprised you, but this doesn't have to be embarrassing. Angel and I only dated four months and it was more than a year ago. He dumped me because he loved another woman. You. And then I met Jared and I fell for him so hard. Angel is my friend. Jared is my heart. Don't hold it against me, okay?"

Julia said nothing, frozen in mortification. The super-friendly

Emily, who Julia was just starting to get comfortable with, was the girlfriend that had made Angel so happy last year. The one that made Julia so jealous that she wrote an erotic romance to channel all her unfulfilled desires. Angel knew all of this and hadn't said a peep. Just left it for her to be blindsided at a big family event. How could she ever look Emily in the eye again?

"Julia? Oh, gosh. I should get Angel."

"No." Julia forced a smile. "I just need a little walk."

"I'll come with you."

She stood. "That's okay. I need a few minutes alone." She headed to the crowded bar area at the far end of the tent so she'd blend in better, not wanting anyone to notice her leaving, and then slipped through the small opening behind it. Off in the distance, she could see the Long Island Sound. It was still afternoon, chilly, but she didn't care, the breeze off the Sound felt wonderful. She slipped off her heels, glad she hadn't bothered with pantyhose, and walked barefoot through the grassy lawn to the rough sand beach and further along to the water's edge, the gently lapping waves soothing her.

She finally stopped at a small rock outcropping and sat, tucking her knees up and wrapping her dress over them. It wasn't that she begrudged Angel for having a girlfriend. She'd told him to find someone else, sure there was no way for the two of them to ever move forward. But to have it sprung on her like this. She'd chatted with Emily at two cooking classes and at the church earlier with Angel nearby. He'd purposely kept this from her all the while knowing two women he'd slept with were getting friendly. Knowing she'd been so jealous she wrote those books! And how did Jared feel about his fiancée sleeping with his brother first? Holy shit. That must've been a doozy. Not a peep about that out of Angel either. The brothers were close, but still, sharing a woman was not something two men did easily. Love didn't work in threes. She should know.

And Angel's family! Did they know Angel slept with Emily? Now it was beyond awkward. Why hadn't Angel told her any of this? That hurt more than anything. She thought they were so close.

She scrambled to her feet. She wanted to go home. Now. She marched back toward the mansion, and then she remembered Angel was her ride. Dammit. She'd get a cab. And she really needed a drink too.

She slipped into the opening of the heated tent and shivered from the sudden temperature change. She stood at the bar, waiting for the bartender's attention. She'd order a shot of whiskey to warm up and take the edge off. That would be the only thing to make the next half hour or so tolerable while she waited for a cab to show up. She wasn't even sure where she was. She had to find out the address.

Jared appeared at her side. "Hi, Julia."

She tensed. "Hi." She really didn't want to talk about this awkward situation with him. She was sure Emily had told him by now. She barely knew him, just talked to him at the one cooking class he'd attended.

"So Emily told me she told you about—"

"It's no problem!" she chirped. Finally the bartender turned her way, and she ordered her whiskey.

She could feel Jared staring at her.

"She didn't mean to, uh, hurt your feelings," Jared said.

"It's fine. No problem." Her whiskey arrived, and she downed it in one shot. She coughed and wiped her eyes.

"It's ancient history," he said.

She met Jared's eyes. Wow, they were so green. "Does everyone know they were together?" she whispered. *And do they know I was so jealous I wrote the Fierce trilogy?*

He dipped his head. "It was kind of obvious when me and Angel had a full-out battle on the front lawn after Sunday dinner."

Her jaw dropped. A full-out battle? And Angel hadn't mentioned any of that either! She clamped her mouth shut. Here she was confiding every little thing, and Angel had this whole other life he never mentioned!

"Uh-oh," Jared said, "you look pissed. It wasn't his fault. Damn. I'm just making this worse, aren't I?" He turned, scanning the crowd just as a man got on a microphone and announced it was time for cake. He turned back to her. "I'll send Angel your way after the cake."

He left.

Julia didn't wait around. She headed into the mansion and out the front door to find the house number and street she was on. Then she went back inside to call a cab. There. Mission accomplished. She felt so damn foolish. And, frankly, mortified. The last to know everything in this obscenely awkward situation.

She heard Angel calling for her. She gritted her teeth and quietly left the foyer, taking a turn down a long hallway. There were paper signs indicating the restrooms were this way. Perfect. She slipped into a bathroom at the end of the wing. The lights flickered on when she entered, so she figured it was just her in here. It had a huge sitting area with wall-to-wall mirrors above a red velvet sofa and matching chairs.

Angel's voice got louder, closer, calling for her. Oh, shit. Why had she hidden in a bathroom? He'd think she was playing along with that Damon fantasy of a public fucking. She was the furthest thing from that now. She should've locked the door.

The footsteps got closer, and she held her breath.

"Julia!" he called and then extremely close, "Julia!" She bit her lip.

The footsteps stopped.

The door swung open to her dark Angel.

Angel stepped inside a bathroom the size of an apartment, locked the door, and, despite what he knew from Jared about Julia being upset, felt a dark desire stirring. Damon and Mia fucking in the closet during a corporate party. Julia showing him her panties. He pushed that desire down, though, when he read the hurt in her eyes. Instead he did the only thing that would make them both feel better—pulled her straight into his arms. She stiffened, which told him she wasn't just hurt, she was pissed off.

He cupped the back of her head and spoke in a low voice near her ear. "You know I dated before we—"

She jerked away. "I'm so embarrassed! Everyone knows but me! They're probably talking about how I'm sitting there, talking to her, with no clue—"

"No one's talking about you, I promise." At her scalding look, he added, "Not anything bad, anyway."

"You saw me with her at cooking class! Twice! You saw us chatting at church and at the reception. You put me next to her on purpose!"

"I had nothing to do with the seating arrangements."

"You and Jared fought over her!"

"Jared fought me. I only defended myself."

Her shoulders drooped. "Why didn't you tell me any of this? I thought we told each other everything."

"Like you told me about the Fierce trilogy?"

She flushed bright pink, but then she rallied. "I called a cab. I'm going home."

"No, you're not."

She crossed her arms. "Yes, I am."

He pushed her arms down and wrapped his arms around her. "It doesn't matter. Emily's in the past."

"She's not in the past! She's in your family!" She shoved at his chest, but he didn't let her get anywhere. "What happens when your family finds out I wrote those books because I was jealous of her?"

A surge of love filled him. He kissed her. She resisted for a moment, so he ramped it up quickly, thrusting his tongue in her mouth and slipping a hand between her legs, excited to find she hadn't put the panties back on. She gasped into his mouth, and then she leaned into his hand. He turned her so her back was to his front, one arm locked around her waist, his hand cupping her sex. "Look at us together."

He gazed at her in the mirror, his dark hair next to her lighter shade, his olive skin pressed cheek to cheek with her fair skin. Her dark blue eyes finally met his in the mirror, halfway between lust and defiance. He felt himself get harder.

He went on. "This is what people see. Two people that belong together. They aren't thinking of who you used to be with or who I used to be with."

"But—"

He dipped his head to nip her neck, a move that always caught her attention. She quieted. "No one will know about your books or why you wrote them unless you tell them." He stroked her lazily, watching her in the mirror. Her lips parted, and her eyes fluttered closed. "I promise you that. Have I ever broken a promise to you?" He increased the pressure over her sweet spot, and her hips rocked mindlessly as little gasps escaped her throat. He let that go on for a while, soaking in her expression of rapturous, sweet surrender before prompting her again. "Answer the question. Have I ever broken a promise to you?"

"You—oh." She shuddered, so close already. "Your promise...so good."

"Come for me," he growled in her ear, and she went off. He loved how she responded to him. He kept stroking her, letting her ride it out. When she finally stilled, he turned her in his arms, and she rested her head on his chest. He ran his hands up and down her sides, reveling in her curves. "We're not done yet."

She lifted her head, her dark blue eyes lit with excitement. He sealed his mouth to hers as he backed her up against the wall. She grabbed for the button on his pants, undoing it and freeing him, wrapping her hand around his hard cock. He managed to get the condom from his wallet, always prepared now that they'd crossed that line, and rolled it on. He hiked up her dress and lifted her leg, fitting himself against her wet heat.

She tore her mouth away. "You said you were going to bend me over." Dammit. She always wanted him to take her from behind. It was her Mia and Damon fantasy, a replay of their guilty weekend of sin.

"I want to see your face when you come." He pressed at her entrance.

She pushed at his chest. "You just saw it in the mirror. Hurry up. They're going to notice you're gone."

He stepped back, though every cell in his body was urging him forward. "What was it that made Mia face Damon, face their future together?"

She turned, bent over, and spread her legs in open invitation, robbing him of any thought beyond burying himself deep. He grabbed her hips and took what she offered, both of them moaning in relief at finally joining. Her soft moans drove him on from a slow screw to a wild, heart-pounding ride. She shuddered around him with a low keening cry that triggered his own explosive release. He closed his eyes, spent, buried deep inside her.

"We should get back," she whispered.

He tightened his grip on her hips, not ready to let her go yet. He needed answers. "Tell me what made Mia face Damon."

She wiggled her hips and peeked at him over her shoulder. "We need to get back."

He didn't release her, instead he pushed deeper. She moaned and dropped her head. "What made Mia face Damon?" he pressed.

"You can't keep me like this." She tried to straighten, and he pushed her back down, pressing her palms against the mirror, entwining his fingers with hers.

"Sure I can," he said. "You turn me on enough to stay buried deep for as long as it takes."

"You're making me mad." But her body said differently, trembling under him.

"Just answer the question. It's just fiction, right?" He did a slow roll inside her that had her breath catching.

"When there were no more secrets between them," she said in a rush.

"And do we have secrets between us?"

She didn't answer. He did another slow roll, and she answered on a shuddering breath. "You know we do."

He stilled, thinking about that. What secrets?

She let out a huffy breath. "If you're not going to fuck me again, let me up."

He pulled out and released her hands. She turned and glared at him as she straightened her dress. He didn't care that she was mad at him. He loved her newly found fighting spirit.

"What secrets?" he asked. They told each other everything. Always had. Well, most everything. Obviously he hadn't told her about Emily specifically, but that was only because he tried not to hurt her by talking about other women, even though she'd always encouraged him to date. And then it occurred to him that maybe she did the same. He clenched his jaw, both not wanting to know and needing to know.

"Not secrets, secret," she muttered.

"Just one?"

She avoided his eyes. "One is plenty."

"Have you been with other men?" he asked through gritted teeth.

She gave him a pained look. "No," she said quietly. "Let's just go."

He racked his brain for what the one secret could be, and then it hit him. The thing that caused her so much shame and regret, them sleeping together and keeping it from Brad. But that wasn't a secret between them. That was a secret between them and Brad. Who wasn't around to tell anymore.

"You mean the secret we kept from Brad about us sleeping together?" he asked just to be sure.

"Yes!" she said like he was extremely dense.

He wanted to say that secret didn't matter anymore, but he knew it did matter. To her.

Before he could figure out the solution, she brushed past him. "I'll leave my panties off as you requested," she said over her shoulder before stepping out into the hallway and quietly shutting the door behind her.

He groaned because he hadn't requested that. Damon did in *Fierce Craving*. He was starting to feel like she really only liked the two of them together as a fantasy. The worst part was, like an idiot, he *did* want to do it again, even knowing he was getting further and further away from what they both really needed.

He shoved his hands in his hair and pulled. How could they release their secret when Brad wasn't around anymore to tell?

15

Twenty-four hours later, Angel was about to lose it. He'd looked at it from every angle, and there was no way to let go of the secret that haunted Julia. It was too late for that. He was mad at Julia for being such a good girl that she was still racked with shame and guilt. He was mad at himself for not just shoving the truth in Brad's face when he had the chance, and he was mad at Brad for getting in between him and Julia.

Besides all that, his stupid hope for the magic of the Italian wedding cookies hadn't happened either. The cookies were gone by the time he and Julia rejoined the wedding reception.

And now he had to get through a rehearsal for Ally's wedding across from Julia, bridesmaid to his groomsman, and somehow not wallow in memories of Julia's wedding knowing what he did now—Julia married Brad out of a sense of duty. And Angel had done nothing to stop it. Somehow he, supposedly an expert at helping people with dysfunctional relationships, had gotten himself into the mother of them all.

And he had no idea how to fix it.

Luckily for Julia, he didn't see her right away when he arrived at Ludbury House. He was somewhere between yelling and shaking her, neither of which would help his cause. Hailey, who he'd quietly dubbed Miss Perky Princess for her sunny personality and pretty looks (even her nose was perky), greeted him in the empty foyer of the large historic house.

"Welcome to Ludbury House!" she exclaimed, rushing up to him with a bright but tight smile. "No time to linger! Up you go to the third room on the right with the other grooms-men." She gestured him up the grand staircase. "Wait for your cue!" she caroled before rushing to the front door to greet the next person.

He stepped into a room full of twentysomething guys he didn't know. They looked like they'd only recently graduated from their college frat. Open snack bags of chips and cans of soda littered the room. "Hey, everyone. I'm Angelo."

He got a series of grunts and chin jerks in return from the guys.

"Which one's the groom?" Angel asked.

Everyone pointed to the guy with shaggy brown hair pacing back and forth. Figured. Angel crossed to Mark. "How're you doing?"

Mark startled and froze, eyes wide. Beads of sweat had formed on Mark's forehead and upper lip like he was danger-ously close to a panic attack.

"You want to take a seat?" Angel asked. "Maybe get a cool drink?"

Mark shifted back and forth on his feet. "No, no, man. I'm cool."

Angel inclined his head and gave the guy some space. He felt like saying *get out while you can! The wedding isn't until tomorrow!* But he knew that was his own shit. He should've said that to Julia before she married the wrong guy.

He looked out the window onto the fallow winter land-scape, remembering the morning of that long-ago wedding. Brad had been a nervous wreck, like Mark, pacing and talking a mile a minute. He'd confessed to Angel in a fit of nerves that he'd lied about being adopted, which Angel had suspected, and asked Angel if he should confess to Julia so he'd start his marriage with no lies between them. Of course Angel had instantly thought of the lie that he and Julia had kept from Brad, the sex weekend that had happened only eight months before, and he'd kept his mouth shut.

But, later, at the reception, Angel thought Brad should come clean. He'd taken him aside and told him he should tell Julia the truth. Because it would hurt her more not to know than it would to know. Unlike the sex lie, which would only hurt Brad to know.

Brad grinned and slapped Angel on the back. "I will, no worries."

"When?" Angel asked.

"Not now, man, it's my big day. Before I ship out. Go find a bridesmaid to hook up with." Brad elbowed Angel in the gut. "I think the redhead's been giving you the eye."

Angel turned just as Julia approached, radiant in her white gown and veil, heading straight for them with a big smile on her face that seemed to take them both in. Brad met her halfway, and Angel took a detour to the bar.

Angel stifled a groan, sick of his Brad memories. He left the room and paced the upstairs hallway, needing to see Julia again, not as a bride, but as a single woman available to him if only he could move them out of Brad's long shadow.

She stepped out of a nearby room with Ally, who was talking excitedly. His eyes were hungry for Julia, taking in every detail as she approached, her soft pink sweater and gray skirt that clung to her curves, her dark brown hair falling in a soft wave over one shoulder. His heart kicked up as her dark blue eyes met his.

She stopped in front of him. "Everything okay?"

He hugged her. "It is now."

She sagged against him. "I thought you were mad at me. When you dropped me off yesterday, you were so quiet." After Luke's wedding and playing out her fantasy one too many times, Angel had been reeling.

He pulled back. "What if I was?"

"Then I'm sorry."

"You don't even know why I'm mad."

"I know. I just hate when you're mad at me, so I preemptively apologize."

He blew out a breath. Weren't they a pair? "I like it better when you fight me."

She gave him a strange look. "You do?"

He whispered in her ear, "It turns me on."

She laughed and whispered back, "Everything turns you on."

"Only you."

She met his eyes in a tender gaze that felt like so much more than lust. This was what he'd been missing. This look in her eyes.

"Julia, I—"

"Hello, everybody!" Hailey caroled, appearing in the hallway with the groom and groomsmen. "Bridesmaids, come out here!"

The women filed out into the hallway.

Hailey beamed at everyone. "Thank you all for coming tonight right on time."

Some of the groomsmen whooped and hollered.

Hailey went on. "The wedding will take place in the foyer with a slow procession by the bridesmaids followed by the bride down the grand staircase. Guys, you will be waiting in the foyer."

Ally linked her arm with the groom's, who was pale. "My dad couldn't make it tonight to walk me down, but he'll be here tomorrow."

"I'll take his place for now," Hailey said. "Groom and groomsmen, places, please."

The guys shuffled down the stairs. The groom swayed on his feet. He hoped Mark didn't pass out on his way down. Angel placed himself just behind the groom as they went downstairs in case he collapsed. They all made it down okay and waited for Hailey to arrange the women.

One day he and Julia would be in a procession just for them. He had to believe it wasn't too late for them. The groom suddenly swayed, and Angel rushed over to steady him. "You okay?" he asked.

Mark turned, sweating profusely. "Yeah. Just got a little dizzy."

He could hear Hailey upstairs bossing the women around, so he figured Mark had a little time. "C'mere," Angel said. "Take a seat and put your head between your knees until it passes." He guided Mark over to a chair in the adjoining parlor room. The other groomsmen started horsing around, loud and obnoxious in the foyer.

Mark sat heavily and put his head between his knees. After a few moments, he lifted his head. "You ever been married?"

"Nope."

"You think this is normal? It's just cold feet, right?"

Angel thought about that. Brad had been a nervous wreck the morning of his wedding, full of anxiety and pacing. But then he thought of his brothers, beaming and enthusiastic, eager to meet their brides at the altar. That was how he would be. If he was about to marry Julia, he'd feel like everything was right in his world. Like their joining together was inevitable just the way their bodies joining together had always been inevitable.

"Do you love her?" Angel asked.

"Sure. Ally's great. And amazing in bed. She got this book—"

"Don't need to know that. I'll get Ally. I'm sure once you talk to her, you'll feel better."

Mark grabbed Angel's arm. "Don't tell her I got cold feet."

"I won't breathe a word." Not that a pacing, sweaty, dizzy Mark wasn't already a dead giveaway. Mark wasn't the sharpest dude in the frat.

He left the groom and joined the women upstairs. Julia looked at him curiously, but he just shook his head and went straight to Ally. "Can you talk to Mark for a minute?"

"Is this important?" Hailey barked. "We need to get through this rehearsal."

"Yeah, it's important," Angel replied.

"Oh, okay," Ally said before rushing downstairs.

Hailey crossed to Julia and gestured Angel over. "I paired you with Julia to walk down the aisle at the end of the ceremony since you two know each other. Okay?"

"Of course," he said, gazing at Julia, who was blushing. It amazed him that she could still blush where he was concerned. But it was probably the fact that all the women were eyeing them speculatively. She didn't like to be the center of attention.

A short while later, Hailey had whipped the groom into shape and lined him up with the groomsmen in the foyer to await the descent of the bridesmaids and the bride. Pachelbel's Canon in D played as the bridesmaids slowly descended the grand staircase to Hailey's enthusiastic refrain of "ooh" and "beautiful" behind them. He watched Julia descend, his heart squeezing at the sight of her.

She met his eyes and smiled, making his heart soar right along with the music. He suddenly wanted to propose to her, just put it all out there. All this wedding stuff was to prepare them for the real deal together. He loved her. He had to tell her. Hopefully she'd feel the same, not just the kind of love between best friends who liked to screw. The forever kind between soul mates.

Julia's gaze shifted to Hailey for Hailey's abbreviated version of the ceremony. Julia had a pleasant expression pasted on her face. This wedding stuff didn't get easier. Probably two weddings in three days was a lot for her.

Hailey was a dynamo, directing everyone while acting as father of the groom and then as mayor joining the bride and groom together.

"I won't sully the sacred vows by repeating them here tonight," Hailey announced. "Instead I will substitute *blah, blah, blah.*"

Everyone laughed.

Finally Hailey was satisfied that they all knew their parts, and they were dismissed. Ally and Mark weren't having a rehearsal dinner. Instead they were heading down the street to Garner's Sports Bar & Grill. Angel had no interest in getting drunk.

He walked out with Julia, holding the large wooden door for her to go ahead of him. She stepped out onto the porch and turned to him.

"You think they'll go through with it?" she whispered. "The groom looked so pale. I thought he might pass out."

Angel chuckled. He couldn't see Mark from where he stood during rehearsal, but he believed it. "I have no idea."

They headed to the back parking lot behind Ludbury House, walking in companionable silence. He walked her to her car as he always did at night. She'd parked close to one of the few lights shining off the back of the house.

She turned to him. "Do you mind that I put you in my stories?"

He stroked her hair and cupped her jaw, leaning down to her ear. "I was extremely flattered to be your fantasy."

She shivered. "I should've checked with you first. I'm sorry. I didn't think anyone would read them or ever know, but…"

"But what?"

"It's catching on more than I ever thought possible. I self-published it, and agents started emailing my pen name. Now I have an agent who's sold foreign rights, paperback rights, and audiobooks. I'm getting a lot of interview requests too."

"Julia, that's great."

"I mean, yes, in some ways it's great. I paid off my parents' debt from all the damage to their house from the last hurricane. I'm saving now too. I figure if I get a five-year cushion, I might be able to do the author thing full time." She frowned.

"But?" he prompted.

"It's exciting, but I really want, no, I *need* to keep my privacy. I don't want people to judge me or you. And I really don't want them to ever find out the truth."

"What's the truth?"

"That I craved you while I was with Brad." The next words came out in a whisper. "Even after my marriage. It's my dirty little secret."

"Then it's my dirty little secret too because I've wanted you since the first day I met you."

Her eyes widened. "What?"

"You didn't know?"

"The first day I met you I cried all over you telling you about the adoption and my mom's death. You wanted me then?"

"Fiercely."

She jolted at the word he'd purposely used because he knew it was powerful for her. She blinked and looked at him in confusion. "But you didn't ask me out. Brad did."

"We both were going to. We fought about it. Brad kissed you before I got the chance, and I guess that turned your head."

She put her fingers over her lips. "That was my first kiss. I was in shock."

"That was your first—" He shoved a hand in his hair. Brad had not been the kind of first kiss Julia deserved. He'd practically shoved his tongue down her throat.

He cradled her face with both hands. "If I'd given you your first kiss, it would've been more like this."

"Ang—"

He sealed his mouth over hers, fitting them together gently, tasting her and pressing a little closer, putting all the love he had for her into it before slowly pulling away. He gazed into her eyes. "Like that."

She blinked, her dark blue eyes wide.

"I love you, Julia. From the very first day we met."

She pulled away. "Don't say that."

"Why not?"

"Because that just means I ruined everything!" she exclaimed.

He pulled her into his arms. "You didn't ruin everything. You just sidetracked it."

She smacked his chest. "Why didn't you tell me back then?"

"I could've done more," he admitted.

"That would've been helpful. I had no clue."

"We were all to blame," he said through his teeth, hating the fact that the past still mattered right now, hating the fact that she didn't say she loved him back.

Her brow furrowed like she was deep in thought. He

pulled back to watch her expression. "What are you thinking?"

She shook her head. "Every time I start to feel good, something happens that sends me reeling backwards again. Those letters, a cold breeze like his ghost, a painful memory. I think Brad wants me to suffer for what I've done. He died a hero. How can I ever live up to that?"

And how could Angel ever live up to that hero bit either?

He blew out a breath in frustration. "I'd better go," he said. "Drive safe."

She gave him a despairing look that broke his heart.

He turned and walked away, one foot after the other, the anguish so overwhelming he went numb. She was right. It was one step forward, two steps back.

And the only person that could truly set them free was gone forever.

～

The next day, Monday, was Valentine's Day, a special day for Julia's students with the exchange of valentines and a party with juice boxes and cupcakes, but for Julia it was nothing but a reminder of all the sweet gifts Brad used to give her— stuffed animals, candy, roses—making every Valentine's Day since a morbid remembrance. She drove home from work, and her thoughts shifted to worry over her friend Ally's wedding later that night. Ally was super excited, almost too excited, especially compared to the groom.

Julia still felt Ally had rushed into the whole thing. Ally was too young, and her fiancé had barely made it through the wedding rehearsal yesterday. He didn't seem mature enough to handle marriage. Julia almost told Ally to cancel. But she held her tongue because Ally seemed so happy and, really, it wasn't like Julia was an expert on marriage.

She'd just pulled into her driveway when her cell phone rang. She'd been getting a lot of calls lately from the realtor about people interested in her house. Julia tried not to be around when people had appointments to tour it.

She grabbed the phone from her purse. "Hello?"

"Hi, is this Julia?" It was a woman's voice, smooth and sultry.

"Who's this?"

"It's Claire Jordan." There was a pause.

Yeah, right. Claire Jordan the hottest actress in Hollywood? Su-u-ure.

"Very funny," Julia said. "I'm hanging up now."

"No, it really is Claire Jordan. From, well, a lot of movies. Have you seen my latest, *Neighborly Attraction*?"

This was not making any sense. How could Claire Jordan be calling her? It must be a prank.

"Julia? Are you still there?"

"How do I know it's really Claire Jordan?"

"Your agent, Milly Wachowski, thought it'd be a nice surprise to hear from me. I loved the Fierce trilogy. I read it twice, and I want to buy the movie rights and star in it."

Julia's vision blurred, suddenly woozy. No one knew her real name behind the pen name, except her agent and Angel. She gripped the phone tighter. "What? You what?"

Claire went on. "I have my own production company. We turn projects around fast. The last book I got rights to I had in theaters eighteen months later. Did you see *Blue Haze*?"

Julia's mouth went dry. Her and Angel on the big screen? Exposed?

"I'm sorry," Claire said after a long silence. "I know this must be a shock. Why is someone you never met calling you, right? I told Milly I wasn't sure you'd like that. I heard you're a very private person and haven't done any press. I could be the face of the Fierce trilogy and do tons of press for you. I don't mind the spotlight." She laughed, a throaty, husky sound.

Julia pressed her fingers to her forehead, willing her brain to work. "How did you find me?"

"I did a little digging, found the agent who handled the sales of your foreign rights, and she was so excited she thought you'd be too. Would you prefer I go through Milly?"

"How much?" Finally her brain was working again. Yes, how much was a good question.

"Three million."

She couldn't find her voice. That was so much more than the five years of take-home pay she was trying to save. That was retire-for-life pay. No-worries-in-the-world pay. Full-time author pay. Her heart raced as the implications sank in.

"Julia?"

"Three million?" she barked. Geez, get a hold of yourself.

"Ah, Milly said you might hold out. The highest I can go is four. And you'll get producer credit."

"Yes," she managed. "Yes. That works."

"Great! I'll have my guy work out the details with Milly. I'm so thrilled. This is the role of a lifetime! When we get a little further along, I'd love to sit down with you and talk about Mia. What makes her tick, make sure I have a good handle on her motivations."

That was when it hit her. How would this affect Angel? It would be very difficult for her to keep a low profile if there was a movie starring Claire Jordan. People might connect the dots between her and Angel, Mia and Damon. At the very least there would be speculation. Angel worked with kids and families in sometimes sticky, personal situations. Would they think he was this dark, dominating character instead of the good man with an alpha streak that he really was? Half the stuff she wrote never happened, it was only her darkest, deepest desires played out.

Claire laughed. "I can see I've pushed the private Julia as far as I'm going to get right now. But I do hope we can talk again. Would that be okay?"

"Yes, yes, of course. Thank you for your call."

"Ciao."

She hung up, somewhere between elation and panic. What should she do? Should she warn Angel? Ask permission? Or would it be possible to keep the whole thing quiet?

She called her agent, Milly, who answered cheerfully. "Hey, it's my favorite author! Did you talk to Claire Jordan?"

"Yes. Please don't spring things like that on me. I'm not exactly smooth off the cuff. I need a heads-up."

"No problem. So what do you think? Movie?"

"I don't know."

"Oh, hold on, now." She squealed. "Just got an email from Claire's production company. The offer is four million. Ooh-eee! Julia, let me call you back. I'm going to see if I can get them to five."

"I—"

Milly hung up.

Julia blinked, staring at her phone as if the answer would be there. She gave herself a mental shake. She didn't have time to sit around pondering. It was already four thirty, and Ally's wedding was at seven. The bridal party had to be there by six. She had to shower and get ready.

She rushed inside the house when it hit her what four or, holy crap, five million could mean for her. The freedom she'd have. She could live anywhere, she could spend her days writing up fantasies. That was the most fun she'd had in her life. And to do that for a living?

She did a little dance.

She'd worry about the consequences later. Right now she was looking at a great opportunity. As long as no one got hurt.

Especially the man who had no idea he'd be starring in a public fantasy in a very big way.

16

Julia showed up early for Ally's wedding at Ludbury House, racing upstairs to the bridal suite. Ally had called her in a crying panic. Julia had bit back what she really thought, that Ally had rushed into things, that she was a child bride much like Julia had been, and instead told her to hang tight, and she'd get there as soon as possible. Ally was simply too young to see past the excitement of being a bride. She found Ally in a puddle of silk and tulle, sobbing, the small veil pinned to her blond hair bobbing in time. The other young bridesmaids were fluttering around her, trying to convince her not to worry.

Julia knelt in front of Ally. "Is it Mark?" She'd thought for sure after yesterday's rehearsal, the groom would bail. Maybe he already had, leaving Ally jilted, all dressed up and nowhere to bride.

"No," Ally sobbed. "It's Dean."

"Your ex?"

"I still love him!" Ally wailed before launching into fresh sobs.

Julia had some experience with this. "Did you tell Dean you still love him?"

"No! I'm hoping it will pass."

"She just has cold feet," Hailey announced, marching into

the room with a determined look on her face. "Ally, all brides go through this nervous, weepy stage. You look gorgeous. Mark is here in his tux, ready to marry the love of his life. So get to the ladies' room, wash up, and I will personally fix your makeup."

Ally nodded and rose to her feet.

"Wait!" Julia said. "Ally, just take a few deep breaths and think about your future. Think about who you want in it. This is forever." Or it was supposed to be.

Ally nodded. "I will. I'll think about it."

Hailey shot Julia a dark look and guided Ally down the hallway to the ladies' room.

"Think she'll go through with it?" a bridesmaid with a bored look asked another bridesmaid.

"I hope so," the other woman replied just as flippantly. "Otherwise I'm spending my Valentine's Day at a wedding for nothing. I could've had a nice dinner out of this."

"The food is supposed to be good here," another bridesmaid said. "Shane O'Hare's catering company is doing it."

"Ooh," the women chorused.

Julia left for a short walk, pacing the upstairs hallway, needing some space. She caught sight of Angel in the foyer, wearing a black tux, looking so handsome. She went to the banister. "Hey, you."

"Hey, darling." He winked. He was in good spirits today. Probably because, though she'd gone home alone last night after their serious talk that depressed the hell out of both of them, he'd showed up at her house an hour later in full alpha mode. Within minutes of entering her house, he'd entered her, taking her against the wall from behind, her hands pinned under his. She got a hot flash remembering. It was damn exhilarating to have her own personal Damon fantasy come to life. Though after, he'd been brusque and quickly left. But how could she complain when he gave her such pleasure and promised to return? Actually what he'd said was, "I can do this for as long as it takes." But, of course, he didn't mean that literally. No man could do that for hours on end, uninterrupted.

The groom and groomsmen were loud and obnoxious, fooling around in the foyer, as young guys could be, but Angel had never been like that. He was a classy guy. People would never look at him the same again if they linked him with Damon. She had to tell him. If Angel said no to the movie, she'd shut down the whole deal. She'd bring it up after the wedding. If there was a wedding.

She raised her voice above the noise. "How's it going on the groom's side?"

Angel gestured to the guys, who were now punching each other for no apparent reason.

She smiled. "It's going like that up here too."

He made a face like an exaggerated *uh-oh*, making her laugh.

"Yeah," she said. "See you in a bit."

An hour later, the bride had pulled herself together with Hailey's help, and the bridal party glided downstairs to the elegant notes of the processional music. She could feel Angel's gaze as she descended the grand staircase just like she'd felt his gaze at her own wedding. Her stomach twisted. She focused on the groom, who was sweating visibly as he recited the wedding vow. She couldn't see Ally's face from where she stood. Was she happy?

The mayor turned to Ally for her turn. "And do you, Allison—"

"I can't do this!" Ally exclaimed, tossing her bouquet and rushing down the small aisle and out the door of Ludbury House. The bouquet of red roses landed at Julia's feet. She picked it up and stared after her friend. The groom ran out the door after his bride.

And then Hailey flipped out. "I'm going to get a bad rep!" She gestured wildly. "Two Valentine's Day weddings can *not* fall through on my watch! They're going to think I'm bad luck!"

She took off after them on tottering high heels.

Julia felt only relief. Now Ally would have her freedom to be with the man she really loved. If Dean actually wanted her back. In any case, Julia hadn't been too impressed with Mark.

She smoothed a petal of a rose. What if Julia had done that? What if she'd declared herself a cheating sinner? What if she'd told Brad about Angel? What if Angel had objected instead of witnessing her marriage?

Angel appeared at her side and smiled. "You caught the bouquet."

"It just sorta fell at my feet."

He glanced around at the chattering guests. "Should we go?"

"Maybe we should stick around in case Hailey persuades them to come back."

"All right. Let's sit down." He gestured toward the back row of the adjacent parlor. They took a seat. The rest of the bridal party wandered toward the back of the house. The small gathering of friends and family in the parlor talked amongst themselves.

What a strange day. First a movie star called her, then she got an offer for millions, and then a runaway bride. She kind of wished she'd had the courage to be a runaway bride too.

"Are you thinking what I'm thinking?" Angel asked.

She searched his expression. "I'm not sure."

"What if you had bailed on your wedding?" he asked.

"What if you had objected?" she returned. "Like when the priest says does anyone object to this marriage?"

His jaw clenched, a muscle ticking in his cheek. She shouldn't have said that. It wasn't his fault.

"I'm sorry," she said.

"Not accepted." He grabbed her arm and pulled her up. "Come on, we're going upstairs to talk privately."

She followed him without protest. They did need to talk. About a lot of things. He led her to the room where the guys had gotten ready. It wasn't nearly as messy as the bridal suite. Just some hangers and dry cleaning bags from the tuxes tossed on a chair and the floor.

Angel shut the door with a bang, and she jumped. "What do you mean if I had objected?"

She shifted uneasily. "I mean—" she swallowed "—what if you said no, I won't be best man. No, Julia, don't marry him."

He advanced on her. "What if *you* said no, I'm not going to marry Brad. I'm going to marry the right guy."

"You never asked me to marry you!"

"How could I? You wouldn't even break up with Brad!"

She stared at the floor. "I couldn't. He was in the hospital."

He stood in front of her and tipped her chin up. "He was out two days later."

She blinked back tears of regret. "I know. I felt too guilty. And then you were gone, and when you finally came back, he was so happy to be with his two best friends. Remember?"

"Yeah, I remember." He dropped his hand. "I remember watching you cuddle up to him and turn your back on me!"

"I never turned my back on you. I always wanted you with us."

"With us! Do you hear yourself? What about with you?"

"I was with Brad. How could I just dump him and go with you?"

"Easy."

"It wasn't easy! He was shipping out—" She lowered her voice. "It doesn't matter. Either way what we did was wrong."

"It was never wrong, Julia! Don't you get that? You were always supposed to be with me!"

"It was never that clear to me!" she cried.

"Fucking A!" he roared. "I fucking hate this, you hear me?"

"Everyone can hear you! Stop yelling at me!"

He kicked a chair, knocking it over. "I'm so sick of this. You want me, you have to come get me." He strode toward the door.

"I'm moving to LA!" she yelled at his back. Where the hell had that come from? But now that she thought about it, that wasn't such a bad idea. No one knew her out there. She could work with the movie people with no judgment, no tie to Angel back home.

He turned. "You're what?"

"They want to make a movie out of my books."

"A movie?" he said so quietly her heart caught in her

throat. He slowly crossed back to her until he was standing in her personal space. "About me and you *fucking*?"

"Maybe no one would figure out it was us."

"Julia." He said her name like she was pure aggravation. He stepped back and crossed his arms. "I could lose my job. I'm on the front lines with kids in crisis. Do you know the kind of man you've made me out to be?"

"I would never mention you. I'd say it was my imagination."

He frowned. "I figured it out after the first chapter." He raised a hand, putting it between them, like he wanted to stop them coming together. "This is the problem with you, Julia. Denial. Big time. When you're ready to own who you are and what you really want, then we can finally be together. In a real, loving relationship. Not just fantasy fucking."

"I don't deserve love!" she cried, and before he could agree with her, she raced out the door.

"Julia!" he called. "Dammit!"

She kept going, down the stairs, out the front door, wanting nothing more than to drive off alone, but when she got to the parking lot, she stopped, her own distress fading in light of the heart-wrenching sight of the bride, Ally, alone and sobbing against a giant oak tree.

She did an about-face and headed over to Ally. "Hey," Julia said gently. "Are you okay?"

"He left."

"Mark?"

"Yes."

"I'm sorry. Did he say why?"

"I told him to go. If I can't have a love like Damon and Mia, then I don't want it."

"Oh, sweetie, that's just fiction. A fantasy."

"That's passion." She wiped her eyes, carefully rubbing the mascara from under them. "I miss it. What I had with Mark wasn't close to what I used to have with Dean."

She knew it! Ally couldn't possibly be over Dean so quickly. They'd dated for four years and Ally had leapt head over ass into her relationship with Mark rather than deal with her grief over the loss of Dean. Julia was sort of an expert on the wallowing in grief thing. "Have you talked to Dean?"

Ally sniffled. "He has a girlfriend. It's too late! I'm screwed! I'm never getting married!"

She put an arm around her and squeezed. "You're young! You've got plenty of time to meet someone. Really. There's no rush."

"All of my friends are getting married!" Ally wailed.

"I'm older than you, and I'm not getting married."

"That's different. You had your bride moment."

Julia bit her lip; the words stung. She had her moment, all right, and it sucked.

"I'm sorry," Ally said. "I shouldn't have said that. I'm not thinking clearly right now."

She shook her head. "No, you're right. I had my moment. You'll have yours. Just not today."

Hailey stormed past, muttering to herself, not seeming to notice them. She got into her bright orange Mini Cooper convertible and sped out of the lot.

"I guess Hailey's upset the wedding didn't happen," Ally said.

"I'm sure there will be many more weddings in Clover Park for her to plan in the future," Julia said.

"Or she'll make them happen," Ally said with a watery smile.

They laughed.

"That does seem to be the way she's heading," Julia said. "You want me to drive you home?"

"No, I can do it. Thanks for listening."

Julia hugged her. "Hey, I give you a lot of credit. I wish I'd had the courage to be a runaway bride."

"You do?"

"Yeah. I was way too young. Nineteen. I was a complete moron, actually."

Ally laughed. "Never. Julia Turner is anything but a moron. You're so put together."

"I'm glad you think that, but I'm just...that's just the

outside. I'm a mess. Hell, I had a spiritual epiphany from a decluttering book."

"I had an epiphany from the Fierce trilogy!"

Julia's smile dropped as her part in this disaster hit home. "Yeah. I guess you did. Take care, Ally."

"Thanks, you too." Ally hugged her again and headed to her car. Julia watched Ally walk briskly through the parking lot, the veil flying out behind her, in considerably better shape than Julia would've been.

Julia headed for her car. Now what kind of epiphany was the Fierce trilogy going to give her? If only it could. That was the problem with being the creator of the stories. She was too close to see anything clearly.

17

———

Julia's thoughts ping-ponged all week on the movie deal. On the one hand, total financial freedom—Milly had gotten the movie people up to 4.5 million. On the other hand, was it really fair to Angel? Because even if she gave him half the money for being her inspiration, he'd still have to deal with the fallout. She hadn't seen him all week, and he'd avoided her at work too. She feared he really was done with her. She replayed their fight at Ally's wedding over and over. He was sick of her and all her issues.

By Saturday she found herself slumped on the sofa, staring at the picture of the three of them—her and Brad and Angel—hoping somehow to find an answer there. She put her hand over Brad. She blinked. She'd never noticed before that she was leaning against Angel's side. There she was squeezed between the two men yet subtly drawn to Angel.

Suddenly she heard Angel's voice in her head *you want me, you have to come get me,* and she realized he'd avoided her this week not because he was done with her, but because he wanted her to take the initiative and go to him. To own what she really wanted. And what she wanted was him. That was what all this Damon-Mia stuff was about. It wasn't just petty jealousy that inspired her fantasy, it was her very real desire to be with him. Why did it take her so long to figure that out? She set the frame back on the shelf, grabbed her coat and purse, and headed to Angel's apartment. It was a former art studio behind a large contemporary-style home. She hadn't been there in a while. He usually went to her place because it was bigger. And ever since she learned Brad had stashed another letter in the baseball card collection he left in Angel's care, she'd avoided visiting. But now all that mattered was seeing Angel.

She knocked on the door and waited, suddenly nervous at what kind of reception she'd get from him.

No answer. Maybe he was still at his Saturday morning tutoring session. She checked the time. He should be back soon. It was nearly noon. She waited in her car on the street out front because it was still cold outside. As soon as she saw his car pull in the driveway, she got out and followed behind him.

He stepped out of his car in his black leather jacket, worn jeans, and briefcase full of papers, and her heart surged with love.

"Hi," she called.

He turned, not seeming surprised to see her. Had he noticed her car and then kept going? He must still be mad at her. "Hey," he said flatly.

"Can we talk?"

"Sure." He opened the door and gestured for her to go in. The apartment was mostly one large space with a kitchen separated by a half wall. Sunlight streamed through the large windows and two skylights. The furniture was simple and functional—a wood dining table with wicker chairs, a futon sofa that pulled out into a bed, an old trunk for a coffee table, and a TV on a small stand.

She dropped her purse and took in his familiar features, so dear to her, yet so closed against her. And that was when she knew what she had to do. "I'm not doing the movie. I'm turning it down."

"Why not?" he asked in a carefully neutral tone.

"I don't want to put you or your job at risk. You were right. It was my own denial that made you into an erotic fantasy because I couldn't deal with my feelings for you in real life."

He crossed his arms, and her chest tightened. He was so distant. Had she lost him for good?

"So you have feelings?" he finally asked.

"Yes," she croaked out over the lump in her throat.

"And how long have you had these feelings?"

Her eyes got hot. "I feel like I've loved you my whole life," she whispered.

"Julia." He pulled her into his arms. "I've loved you since the day we met."

"I'm so sorry I ruined everything."

He stroked her hair. "Things got fucked up, but we're here together." He tilted her chin up to look at him and kissed her gently. "It's not too late."

She threw herself against his chest, hugging him tightly. "I thought I lost you."

"You could never lose me. Don't you know that by now? You've got my heart." He kissed the top of her head. "I was just giving you some tough love."

"It worked."

He pulled back. "Listen, I want you to do that movie. They're probably offering a lot of money, right?"

"Four point five million."

He staggered back. "Whoa. You were going to leave that on the table for me?"

She nodded.

He grabbed her and spun her around. "Take it! We'll live together off the money. I won't have to be a social worker. You won't have to be a teacher. I know you always dreamed of being an author."

"But what would you do?" she asked.

"Maybe I'll go back to school and get my PhD in psychology. Or maybe I could be your manager. Handle the public for you. I don't know. We'll figure it out."

"And you don't mind if people think you're Damon?"

"Hell, it's a compliment. I'm a fucking stallion."

She laughed. "But I thought you were worried what people would think of you."

"As a social worker with sensitive client information on kids. But if I do something else, maybe working with adults, or just working with you, it'll be fine."

Hope surged through her heart. "Where would we live?"

"Here. Home. We'll buy a house together." He gestured around him. "This place is too small for a big-time author."

She glanced around at his studio apartment, neat as ever. Her gaze caught on the old trunk Angel used as a coffee table. He'd had that trunk back at college too, which reminded her of Brad's letter. She needed to get that out of the way. "Do you still have Brad's baseball card collection?"

He suddenly looked wary. "Yeah, why?"

"There's a letter in the bottom of the box. We're supposed to read it together."

Angel let out a long sigh. "Julia."

"Never mind. We don't have to read it."

"I just don't want you going off the deep end again. I finally got you to admit you have feelings for me."

"I love you." Her entire body tingled, giddy with the love she felt and could finally express. She smiled widely and burst out in a laugh at the wonder of it all.

Angel beamed and gave her a quick hug. "I love you too. Alright. I'll read the letter. And if I think it won't upset you, I'll give it to you to read too. Deal?"

She nodded. She trusted Angel to look out for her. The last thing she wanted was another bomb dropped on her from Brad. Last time he'd confessed he'd lied about being adopted. What would he say next? *Hey, guess what? I was gay all along.* She really couldn't handle any more confessions.

Angel went straight to the trunk and opened it. Whoa. It was like she'd sensed the letter was in there. He pulled out a cardboard box, closed the trunk, and set it on top. His mouth tightened almost imperceptibly before he opened the box and took out the preserved baseball cards that were probably worth something by now. Finally, he muttered, "Fucking A."

He carefully retrieved the envelope, opened it, and pulled

out a picture and a letter on the same lined paper as the other two letters. Angel sank to the sofa and stared at the picture. She couldn't breathe for a moment. What was it? Angel set the picture face-down on the sofa and unfolded the letter. She watched his expression as he read, looking shell-shocked. She bit her lip. It must be bad.

She couldn't stand the suspense. "What is it?"

"C'mere."

She sat at his side, and he handed her the picture. Oh! It was her and Angel on New Year's Eve. Angel had kissed her on the cheek, and Brad had snapped the picture as she beamed, eyes closed, taking it in. The love between her and Angel was clear as day. "I remember this. Our first New Year's. Brad was so drunk."

"Read the letter," he said, his voice gravelly.

She set the picture back on the trunk and took the letter from his hand. She closed her eyes, taking a deep, calming breath. It couldn't be that bad, right? Angel wouldn't let her get hurt anymore over this. But he seemed so shell-shocked. Angel put a reassuring hand on her leg, giving it a gentle squeeze. She opened her eyes and read:

Dear Julia and Angel,

Surprise, you cheating rat bastards! I knew. I always knew. When I got back to school after that long bout with mono, Angel made himself scarce. Not easy to do given we had two classes together, and a dead giveaway. And, Julia, you were so sad, though you tried to hide it. And neither of you would tell me what the hell happened. I put two and two together. Give each other a good hard glare from me. There. Feel better? Yeah, I was pissed, but I forgave you, both of you, because I knew Angel wanted you from the start, and I moved in on you anyway. Julia, I've always been a screwup, but I wanted to be the man you deserved, so I joined the army. I wanted to be what Angel was all along—strong, steady, everything done out of some deep good place inside like I wished I had. I know you liked my pretty face and my pretty patter, but it was always a sham. A cover-up for what I lacked. I asked Angel to look after you if I didn't make it back. I know if you're reading this, he did. Thank you, Angel, from the bottom of my heart. I can never repay you for all that you've done. I bought the house in Fieldridge so Julia could stay close to you. I wanted you to be together (if I was gone). I love you guys. Maybe now you'll have the chance to be the matched set you were always meant to be.

Love,
Brad

P.S. Kiss her, pretty boy! And take the money from the sale of the Fieldridge house and buy your own house together. Fuck, do I have to do everything?

She slapped a hand over her mouth. She couldn't believe it. He knew. All those years he knew, and he forgave them. Angel's eyes were watery. She threw her arms around him, and they just held each other as the sun streamed through the skylight above them, bathing them in healing afternoon light.

After a while, the sun on Julia's cheek burned, unusual for February. She glanced at the sky, where a few sunbeams shone through the clouds like a hand reaching down from heaven. Maybe it was Brad in one last goodbye. She buried her face in Angel's chest. Even Brad knew they were a matched set. Soul mates.

Finally she lifted her head to gaze into the eyes of the man she loved. Angel kissed her tenderly and cupped her face with both hands. "My Julia, *finally* and at long last, will you marry me?"

"Yes!" she cried and then they were kissing, and the rest was a hot blur of clothes flying. They fell to the sofa, the letter fluttering to the floor, freeing them to be together as they were always meant to be.

EPILOGUE

Angel was eager to bring Julia to Sunday family dinner the next day. Finally he wouldn't be the only bachelor in his band of besotted brothers. Finally he could make the love of his life a permanent part of the family. If only Julia would *finally* pick an outfit.

"What do you think of this?" she asked, appearing in the living room in her fifth outfit of the night. She wore the soft dark blue sweater he loved because of the way it clung to her breasts and a gray skirt. The skirt could've been a little tighter but…

"Perfect," he said.

She fluttered her hands in the air. "No. I saw your face when you looked at the skirt. This won't do." She turned and went back into the bedroom.

He scrubbed a hand over his face. "Julia," he called, "we're going to be late. All of those outfits were perfectly fine." He knew she was nervous, but, at this rate, they were going to miss dinner completely. She'd met everyone at Luke's wedding, but she hadn't actually said more than the briefest of greetings both because she was embarrassed about the Emily situation and because everyone had been so busy dancing and celebrating.

She marched back out in just the sweater and some

matching blue panties that had him perking up. "This is important! I'm sure they're going to have a lot of questions about me and are wondering why we haven't been together after all these years." She bit her lip. "They'll probably feel sorry for me for being a widow—"

"Stop." He stood and crossed to her. "They're going to love you." He kissed her long and deep until she melted against him. He pulled away and met her dark blue eyes. "No one's going to ask you any hard questions, I promise."

She hugged him tight. "Did you warn them I'm the author of the Fierce trilogy?"

"No. That's up to you when you want to tell people."

She pulled away. "I'll wait until the last possible minute."

"No-o-o, that doesn't sound like you," he teased.

She pursed her lips. "For both our sakes. If the movie really happens, and Milly thinks it will, we can both give notice, finish out the school year, and then tell everyone."

"That sounds like a plan."

She brightened. "It does, doesn't it? We should get married in June when the school year ends."

"Done."

She beamed and went back to the bedroom to change. A few moments later she emerged, still wearing the clingy blue sweater with a form-fitting black skirt.

"Yes!" he exclaimed. "Perfect! I love it!"

Her eyebrows shot up at his unusual enthusiasm for her outfit. He never cared what she wore. If he had his way, she'd be naked all the time. But now, they really had to go. He took her by the hand and pulled her to the door.

"Wait, my coat!" she said. "I need the nice one."

He snagged the long black wool coat and her purse where he'd already left it by his coat and ushered her out the door.

"You would have liked whatever I put on next, wouldn't you?" she asked once they were in the car.

He gave her a devilish smile. "I always just imagine you naked, so it really doesn't matter."

Her cheeks colored pink, which he found adorable,

knowing her complete abandon in the bedroom. He gave her a smacking kiss on the mouth. "We're outta here."

He made the short drive to his oldest brother Gabe's house in Clover Park. Julia was quiet on the way over, and he didn't disturb her silence with a lot of talk. He knew she'd have enough of that the moment they stepped into the house with his large family.

When he parked out front, he could tell by the cars that everyone was already there. He didn't want to disturb the meal, so he just let himself in the unlocked front door. A gray and silver furball charged into the foyer, barking like crazy.

"Hey, Fred," Angel said, rubbing the dog behind the ear.

Fred quieted then turned to Julia and tried to get his nose up her skirt. Angel shoved Fred's head away.

"There you are!" Zoe exclaimed, rushing to greet them. She was Gabe's wife, a bubbly woman with bright brown eyes. She stopped in front of Julia and held her by the arms. "So good to see you again! We're so happy you're here!"

Julia flushed bright pink. "Thank you. I'm happy to be here."

"Here, let me take your coats," Zoe said. "I'm Zoe, in case you don't remember in the sea of faces you met at the wedding. And p.s. there's a lot of people who can't wait to see you!"

Julia grabbed his hand in a tight grip. He led her to the dining room, where his whole family was sitting—his dad, his stepmom, his five brothers, his sisters-in-law, and toddler Miles. Surprisingly, the food on the table—two trays of lasagna, garlic bread, and tossed salad—was untouched.

"You guys," he said, "you didn't have to hold up dinner for us."

His brothers stared at Julia in open curiosity. His sisters-in-law were more subtle, each of them smiling at her, but checking her out just the same. Julia's pink cheeks were nearing scarlet territory with all the attention on her.

His dad stood and shook Julia's hand. "So good to see you again, Julia. Welcome."

His stepmom appeared on Julia's other side and

enveloped her in a warm hug. "I can't tell you how much it means to us that you came to Sunday dinner."

Just wait until they told them they were getting married. He'd saved that for an in-person announcement.

Julia swallowed visibly. "I'm sorry it took me so long."

"Not at all," his dad said. "Please, have a seat."

Jared indicated the empty seats next to Miles, who now sat at the table with a booster seat. Julia rushed over and sat right next to Miles.

Angel stopped behind her. "Don't sit there. Take the other seat."

She shot him a dark look over her shoulder. "Angel, it's fine. I love babies." She leaned close to Miles. "And what's your name?"

Splat! Miles gifted Julia with a handful of what appeared to be banana pudding, mostly on her nose but dripping down quickly to her mouth and chin. The yellow clashed with the red of her face as she grabbed a napkin to wipe it off.

"I told you," Angel said, stifling a laugh.

The men were all biting back smiles; the women glared at their men.

"Ah!" Zoe exclaimed as she returned to the dining room after hanging up their coats. "I am *so* sorry! He won't stop throwing food." She rushed over and tried to wipe Julia's face with a napkin, but Julia leaned back.

"It's okay," Julia said. "I got it. Can you just show me to the powder room?"

"Of course."

Julia left with Zoe, and Angel felt the first twinge of guilt as silence descended on his usually noisy family.

He took the seat in the food-throwing zone himself. "Not cool," he told Miles.

"I'll get him," his stepmom said. She scooped up Miles and set him on her lap. "We are going to learn some manners, young man."

She'd be the one to instill them, for sure. She'd brought them all up with good manners and taught them to be respectful, even if his brothers were a little rough around the edges.

"So does this mean you're together?" Emily asked.

He smiled. "Yes, we're together. I wouldn't have brought her if it wasn't serious."

"It's serious," his stepmom whispered to his dad.

The room went quiet as Julia returned, all eyes on her. The pink immediately returned to her cheeks. Might as well get the big announcement out of the way since she was already the center of attention.

He stood and met her halfway. "I love you," he said, which was the only warning she'd get.

She beamed and said softly, "I love you too. But shouldn't we sit down? Nobody's eating. I think they're waiting for us."

He put his arm around her shoulders and turned to his family, who were all gazing at them curiously. "We're getting married in June."

His stepmom let out an audible gasp and then everyone spoke at once, congratulating them. The women rushed to Julia, hugging her and welcoming her to the family. His brothers slapped him on the back, bowling him over with their enthusiasm. It was crazy joyful chaos.

Finally all the excitement settled down enough for everyone to go back to the table to eat.

"Wait a minute," Jared said. "Me and Emily are getting married in June. It's...when is it, Em?"

"June fourth," Emily said dryly.

"Yeah," Jared said, "I knew it was early."

"And I'm due June seventeenth," Sophia said, putting a hand on her baby bump. Vince's wife was five months along.

Nico's wife, Lily, piped up. "I'm due June twenty-fifth." They were both expecting girls, and he had a feeling they'd be as close as twins.

Julia turned to him with a smile. "We're going to need a coordinator to work out all the logistics. I think Hailey just got her first big wedding."

He grinned. "It's going to be a helluva June for our family."

"Hear, hear!" his dad said, raising his glass. Everyone raised their glass. "To family."

"To family," they all chorused. They clinked glasses all around and drank.

"I want to start our family right away," Julia announced, shocking him. First because she was such a private person, and second because they hadn't even talked about it.

Another round of cheers and congratulations went around.

She turned to him. "Is that okay? I feel like we've lost so much time. I don't want to wait."

"It's more than okay." He kissed her tenderly, and she gave him a loving look in return that warmed him all the way to his toes.

"I love you so much," she whispered.

"I love you so much too," he said.

"Damn," Vince boomed. "And she didn't even eat the cookies."

"I did," Angel said, trying to spare his stepmom's feelings, who truly believed her Italian wedding cookies were the key to marrying off her sons.

"She will," his stepmom said. "They're waiting for us for dessert."

"Better get one, Ma," Vince said. "Don't let her get away."

"You're absolutely right," she said, handing Miles over to his grandfather. "I'll be right back."

A few moments later, his entire family watched while Angel fed Julia an Italian wedding cookie. It meant a lot to his stepmom. For Angel it was just good luck.

Julia chewed and swallowed while everyone stared at her expectantly, though he had no idea what they thought she might say. They'd already announced a wedding in June.

She grinned at him. "I think I just got pregnant!"

Everyone laughed.

"She's going to fit in here just fine," his dad said. "Now let's eat."

∼

Julia and Angel's wedding had been a *long* time coming, and it was finally here. Julia had wanted elegant and sophisticated at Clover Park's Ludbury House, a black-tie affair befitting the joining of the love of her life, and that was exactly what she got. She paid for it herself with the money from selling the movie rights. Over the last few months, she'd grown very close to her new sister-in-law Emily as they both excitedly planned for a June wedding (Emily's wedding was a week before Julia's). Emily was the sister Julia had always wanted. They'd even gone dress shopping together. Hailey was, of course, ecstatic to help plan Julia's wedding, especially once she heard that the movie star Claire Jordan would be attending.

Filming on the Fierce trilogy would begin in August, and Claire had been spending the past couple of weeks in Clover Park, hanging out with Julia and Angel, and digging deep for her character. They hadn't told her the characters were based on them, but Claire picked it up within minutes of their first meeting with her. "Omigod, it's you! You're Mia! The attraction is electric! Oh, this is even better! Now I can get in both your heads."

Julia made Claire put it in writing that their identities would never be revealed before she'd say another word. Once they'd worked that out, she and Angel continued their conversation with Claire. Strangely enough, Julia's forceful-ness turned Angel on. Hell, lately, most everything did. In any case, the night after she stood up to the glamorous Claire Jordan, Angel insisted they act out the dining room table scene from *Fierce Longing*. It was so dirty. And multiple orgasm, limp-as-a-ragdoll good.

Besides Claire, they'd invited everyone in the singles book club to their wedding, the teachers and principal from work, her parents, and Angel's whole family. His family had taken both her authorship and her Damon inspiration in stride. In fact, they were actually very proud and supportive of them both. Her own parents were still in shock. She did have a bit of a girl-next-door vibe, she knew, and her parents were trying to reconcile that image with reality.

She and Angel had put in their resignations at work and finished out the school year the week before the wedding. The timing couldn't be helped. They had Jared and Emily's wedding the first weekend in June and didn't want to risk having their own wedding any later in case Sophia and Lily went into labor. As it was, both women were bursting, nine months along with the daughters they carried. She and Angel had agreed to start trying for a baby on their wedding night. She knew he'd be a fantastic dad and couldn't wait to have their own little family.

Her house had sold, and she'd moved into Angel's place. They were still house hunting, but were hoping for a contemporary-style house like Julia had always wanted. Lately, Angel had been scouting around for some land so they could build their dream home together. They planned on staying close to his family, wanting the cousins to grow up together.

Julia stood alone now in the bridal suite of Ludbury House, at her request for a moment's quiet before the ceremony. She looked in the mirror and beamed, bursting with happiness. The gown was modern, a flowing white satin with color blocked silver on the bottom. She turned and admired the keyhole back with rows of crystal swags. Glimmering buttons ran all the way to the train. She wore no veil, preferring to face Angel with nothing between them. Her hair was swept up in a twist with tendrils of loose hair on either side of her face. But it wasn't the gown or the hair or makeup that made her feel radiant. She'd forgiven Brad, and Brad had forgiven her. Her heart was open to all the love she had for Angel, and his for her. Which was an overwhelming mushy lot.

Hailey burst back in the room, clipboard in hand. "Did you have your quiet moment?"

Julia smiled indulgently. "Yes, I'm good." She knew it had killed Hailey to give her that moment. She'd been fluttering around like a crazed butterfly ever since they arrived, fretting over the flowers and getting the details right. The details that Julia had thrilled to plan, so different from her first wedding, everything that suited her and Angel here and now. Hailey didn't have to worry. Everything was perfect.

The bridesmaids and groomsmen—Angel's brothers and sisters-in-law plus her friends, Ally and Gina, walked in pairs down the grand staircase first. Sophia and Lily, practically waddling at nine months, had opted out of the bridal party. They relaxed in cushioned chairs along with the other guests in the large foyer. More people stood on either side of the foyer, watching from the large parlor and formal living room. Julia hadn't wanted her father to give her away. She wanted her and Angel to be partners as they joined together.

Finally it was their turn. Angel, looking gorgeous in a black tux, met her in the upstairs hallway, seeing her in the gown for the first time. A smile played over his lips as he took her in from head to toe. His dark brown eyes were full of love as they gazed into hers. He kissed her cheek before whispering, "You look beautiful. Are you nervous?"

She beamed. "Not at all. Nothing has ever felt so right."

He blinked, his eyes watering. "I couldn't agree more," he said in a choked voice.

"Don't start that," she warned, fighting back her own tears. "I need to hold it together. Hailey will kill me if I mess up my makeup."

He laughed. The music started. He leaned close, offering his arm to her like he had the first time they'd met. And this time, she took it, absorbing his warmth and steadiness, the rightness of the gesture zinging down to her toes. They descended the grand staircase together.

All eyes were on them, but all Julia could think of was saying the vows. She'd written her own and they would be a surprise gift for Angel. The crowd was hushed as the ceremony began. The mayor of Clover Park was acting official. Angel went first, reciting the traditional vow, promising in a voice full of pure love and solid intentions to love her in sickness or in health, for richer or poorer, for the rest of his days.

"The bride has written her own vows," the mayor said.

Angel didn't blink at the surprise, he took most things in stride, and only said warmly, "Julia."

She swallowed over the lump in her throat. The hardest part would be getting all the words out without breaking down in tears. She took a deep breath. "Angelo Marino, you have been my other half, my soul mate, my best friend, and so much more from the first day we met. I will spend the rest of my life dedicated to your happiness." She paused. "I was lost for so long, and you were my rock. Now I want to be that for you, for richer or poorer, sickness or health, all the highs and lows that life brings, I bind myself to you, body, heart, and soul for eternity. Not even death will ever part us." A tear escaped and Angel brushed it away with his thumb. "I look forward to a long life with you, to our children and grandchildren, and to the happy harmonious home we will make together."

Angel's eyes were watery when she finished. "Thank you, darling."

She blinked and another tear escaped. She nodded, unable to speak.

The mayor jumped in and quickly proclaimed them husband and wife. She threw her arms around Angel's neck and kissed him with all the love in her heart. The crowd cheered, and when she turned to beam at their family and friends, she was surprised to see so many wiping tears from their eyes.

They accepted congratulations from everyone before Hailey hustled them down the hallway to the reception in the large ballroom at the back of Ludbury House. The curtains were closed, the room lit with crystal chandeliers and glowing votive candles set on long tables holding refreshments. The press hovered around the property, hoping to catch sight of Claire Jordan and the reclusive author of the new movie franchise, but Hailey had kept everything on the inside of Ludbury House private.

They danced, they celebrated, they loved. Julia had never felt so happy, her future with Angel so bright.

Hailey finally calmed down near the end of the reception, hugging them both and congratulating them. Josh, the bartender from Garner's, was Hailey's date, but Hailey didn't seem to see him as a romantic interest so much as an assistant. Josh had a bit of a badass biker vibe to him, which made him look especially comical in a tux, holding Hailey's purse. Hailey was still busy with her clipboard, checking off items for the reception and making sure everything was going according to schedule.

"Are you two ready for the big send-off?" Hailey asked Julia and Angel.

"Yup." Angel grinned. They were heading from here straight to the airport for a honeymoon in Paris. Angel was going all out on the romantic stuff. He said he had to make up for lost time.

"I can't wait," Julia said. "I've never been to Paris."

"Me either," Angel said.

Hailey sighed happily. "You two are so cute. I have got to get more sweet couples like you in here." She turned to Josh. "I get credit for this one. If it wasn't for my singles book club, these two wouldn't have gotten together."

"Uh—" Angel started.

"Save your breath," Josh said with a laugh.

Not that Hailey noticed. She was beaming as if she was solely responsible for any love that took place in Clover Park. She looked up at Josh. "Do you have any brothers?"

One corner of his mouth lifted. "Not any that you'd like to meet."

"Why not?" Hailey demanded.

He paused, a twinkle in his eye, before finally saying, "I'm the good one."

Hailey lit up. "Are they bad boys? I can reform them! Women love bad boys."

"The baddest," Josh said wryly.

Hailey gasped. "You mean, criminals?"

"Worse."

"What could be worse than criminals?"

"Wouldn't you like to know." Josh turned to Julia and Angel. "Congrats. Enjoy Paris."

"Thank you," Julia said.

Angel shook Josh's hand. "Thanks."

Josh turned and left. Hailey hurried after him, demanding to know about his brothers.

"He's in trouble," Angel said.

Julia laughed. "She'll make him talk."

Angel kissed her. "Come on, Mrs. Marino, it's time for us to start our new life together."

"I like the sound of that."

They walked out the door, hand in hand, more than ten years after the day they'd first met, and never too late.

Would you like to find out more about Hailey, Josh, and all the future weddings she has planned? Check out my spinoff Happy Endings Book Club series! Get started with book 1, *Hidden Hollywood*.

Want more Clover Park series? Discover where the Marino-Reynolds family began in *A Valentine's Day Gift*, Allie and Vinny's story! They're the parents of the Marino-Reynolds family. Plus, you'll get a peek at their sons when they were still pups!

A Valentine's Day Gift

When Allie Reynolds strikes up an unlikely friendship with the contractor working on her house, Vinny Marino, she never expected how much he'd come to mean to her. So much separates them it seems impossible—he's mourning his late wife, she's trapped in a loveless marriage. Will they make the tough choices to give themselves a chance at love? Or will responsibility keep them from their happy ending?

Sign up for my newsletter and never miss a new release! https://www.kyliegilmore.com/newsletter

ALSO BY KYLIE GILMORE

Unleashed Romance <<steamy romcoms with dogs!

Fetching (Book 1)

Dashing (Book 2)

Sporting (Book 3)

Toying (Book 4)

Blazing (Book 5)

Chasing (Book 6)

Daring (Book 7)

Leading (Book 8)

Racing (Book 9)

Loving (Book 10)

The Clover Park Series <<brothers who put family first!

The Opposite of Wild (Book 1)

Daisy Does It All (Book 2)

Bad Taste in Men (Book 3)

Kissing Santa (Book 4)

Restless Harmony (Book 5)

Not My Romeo (Book 6)

Rev Me Up (Book 7)

An Ambitious Engagement (Book 8)

Clutch Player (Book 9)

A Tempting Friendship (Book 10)

Clover Park Bride: Nico and Lily's Wedding

A Valentine's Day Gift (Book 11)

Maggie Meets Her Match (Book 12)

The Clover Park Charmers series <<sweet and sexy charmers!

Almost Over It (Book 1)

Almost Married (Book 2)

Almost Fate (Book 3)

Almost in Love (Book 4)

Almost Romance (Book 5)

Almost Hitched (Book 6)

Happy Endings Book Club Series <<the Campbell family and a romance book club collide!

Hidden Hollywood (Book 1)

Inviting Trouble (Book 2)

So Revealing (Book 3)

Formal Arrangement (Book 4)

Bad Boy Done Wrong (Book 5)

Mess With Me (Book 6)

Resisting Fate (Book 7)

Chance of Romance (Book 8)

Wicked Flirt (Book 9)

An Inconvenient Plan (Book 10)

A Happy Endings Wedding (Book 11)

The Rourkes Series <<swoonworthy princes and kickass princesses!

Royal Catch (Book 1)

Royal Hottie (Book 2)

Royal Darling (Book 3)

Royal Charmer (Book 4)

Royal Player (Book 5)

Royal Shark (Book 6)

Rogue Prince (Book 7)

Rogue Gentleman (Book 8)

Rogue Rascal (Book 9)

Rogue Angel (Book 10)

Rogue Devil (Book 11)

Rogue Beast (Book 12)

Check out my website for the most up-to-date list of my books:
kyliegilmore.com/books

ABOUT THE AUTHOR

Kylie Gilmore is the *USA Today* bestselling author of over fifty humorous contemporary romances. Her series include Unleashed Romance, the Rourkes, the Happy Endings Book Club, Clover Park, and Clover Park Charmers. With more than three million downloads of her books, readers all over the world love escaping into her hilarious feel-good romances featuring strong bonds with family, friends, and community.

Kylie lives in New York with her family, a demanding cat, and a nutso dog. When she's not writing, reading hot romance, or dutifully taking notes at writing conferences, you can find her flexing her muscles all the way to the high cabinet for her secret chocolate stash.

Sign up for Kylie's Newsletter and get a FREE book! kyliegilmore.com/newsletter

For text alerts on Kylie's new releases, text KYLIE to the number (888) 707-3025. (US only)

For more fun stuff check out Kylie's website https://www.kyliegilmore.com.

Thanks for reading *A Tempting Friendship*. I hope you enjoyed it. Would you like to know about new releases? You can sign up for my new release email list at https://www. kyliegilmore.com/newsletter. I promise not to clog your inbox! Only new release info, sales, and some fun giveaways.

I love to hear from readers! You can find me at:
kyliegilmore.com
Instagram.com/kyliegilmore
Facebook.com/KylieGilmoreToo
Twitter @KylieGilmoreToo

If you liked Angel and Julia's story, please leave a review on your favorite retailer's website or Goodreads. Thank you.